Also by Ron Schwab

The Lockes

Last Will
Medicine Wheel
Hell's Fire

I0672574

The Law Wranglers

Deal with the Devil
Mouth of Hell
The Last Hunt
Summer's Child
Adam's First Wife
Escape from El Gato
The Prince of Santa Fe
Peyote Spirits

The Coyote Saga

Night of the Coyote
Return of the Coyote
Twilight of the Coyote

The Blood Hounds

The Blood Hounds
No Man's Land
Looking for Trouble
Snapp vs. Snapp

Lucky Five

Old Dogs
Day of the Dog

Lockwood
The Accidental Sheriff
Beware a Pale Horse
Trouble

Sioux Sunrise
Paint the Hills Red
Grit
Cut Nose
The Long Walk
Coldsmith
Ghost of the Guadalupe
Bushwa
Blizzard

Unbroken

Ron Schwab

Uplands Press

OMAHA, NEBRASKA

Uplands Press
1401 S 64th Avenue
Omaha, NE 68106
www.uplandspress.com

Uplands Press / Ron Schwab -- 1st ed.
ISBN 978-1-943421-76-3

Unbroken

Chapter 1
The Summons

SECOND LIEUTENANT HENRY Ossian Flipper was an 1877 graduate of West Point and had been trained in the art of war and the use of virtually every weapon utilized in combat. Now, in late spring of 1880, he was an experienced officer but with only a few exceptions he had mostly flirted with danger but not faced it head on.

Assigned to Fort Davis in southwest Texas now, he and hundreds of other cavalrymen were scattered about the rugged, semi-arid country southwest of the Pecos River. Months earlier, Flipper, with several troops of colored Tenth Cavalry "Buffalo Soldiers," had accompanied a wagon train from Fort Sill to southwest Texas before continuing to their new posting at Fort Davis.

His troop had just broken camp and saddled up under a clear morning sky. The rolling prairie lands ahead of the column would be the perfect subject for a landscape painting, Flipper thought. The sky displayed multiple hues of blue as the sun climbed over the horizon and dropped shadows over the random stone formations and desert brush and revealed an array of colors on stony land surface. Of course, the artist would be forced to work quickly before he suffocated in the heat that was on its way.

He signaled his small troop to a halt when he saw a rider heading their direction in a whirlwind of dust, pushing his mount harder than the young lieutenant liked to see. When the rider arrived and reined in, Flipper saw that he was a young, fuzzy-cheeked private with blond hair pasted by sweat to his forehead beneath the bill of his cap.

The private saluted Flipper. "Private Cooper Swenson, sir. I am a courier from Colonel Benjamin Grierson. He sent me to inform Lieutenant Henry Flipper of his plight."

Flipper returned the salute. "I am Lieutenant Flipper. What is the colonel's plight? I left him on his way to Eagle Springs not more than two days ago." The colonel had been checking on troops in the field and was generally accompanied by a good number of cavalrymen, but he often sent units out on missions and had ordered Flipper's own troop to return to Fort Davis with a report and new orders for the acting commanding officer there.

Private Swenson said, "Sir, Colonel Grierson had only eight men surrounded by Apache in a canyon to the southwest when I rode out after dark last night. The Apache started to follow us soldiers and the ambulance wagon late afternoon yesterday and kept adding to their numbers. I ain't ashamed to say I was dang scared about finding my way through them Injuns. But somehow, I did it. I'm praying the colonel picked up ten more men."

"How would that happen?"

"Some hours out, I was pretty much lost, and it had turned dark as a cave. I wandered around and saw a firelight. Hoping it wasn't Apache, I headed that way, and I stumbled on a camp with a patrol of Tenth Cavalry soldiers. I told the sergeant—don't recollect his name—who I was looking for and he sent me this way. The sergeant was going to see if he could get his patrol to the colonel."

Colonel Grierson had given Flipper several scouting missions to complete on his way back to Fort Davis, and that was why he would have known the officer was not far away. Half of Flipper's troop had split off earlier under a sergeant's command on a scouting quest, leaving Flipper with only fifteen cavalrymen. He and Sergeant Murphy had agreed upon potential rendezvous locations, so the sergeant could have made a good guess at Flipper's location. Private Swenson got lucky. A lot of that might be needed today, but Flipper never counted on luck.

He assumed the Apache were Chiricahua or Mescalero, likely a war party from Victorio's Warm Springs band. The band had attacked a picket of a dozen soldiers some forty miles south of Fort Davis in southwest Texas a week earlier, killing three and wounding several others. Several settlers' families had been burned out by Apache who spared none from the scalping knives.

Troops and scouting parties from Fort Davis were chasing all over the area trying to capture the renegades and return them to the reservations. Flipper saw this as a predictably futile effort given that the Apache were divided into many bands and war parties and knew this barren land far better than any soldier. The best hope, he figured, was to inflict enough damage to the war parties that they would pull back and retreat, probably to Mexico, and eventually decide that the reservation was their wisest choice.

Before leading his small troop out, he ordered his troopers to dismount and water their horses at the nearby stream. He did not know when they might find water again. He spoke with the courier as they stood between their two mounts, Flipper standing nearly two inches over six feet and towering over the shorter private.

Flipper said, "Private Swenson, I can't offer you any rest. We need you to lead us to Colonel Grierson, but we've got a fresh horse to give that gelding some rest. Now, tell me where the colonel and his men were when you last saw them."

"Yes, sir. We'd made a stop for water at a spring in a little canyon. Dusk was a few hours away, and considering the Injuns we saw, the colonel figured we'd go another few hours and try to find a place to fort-up. The Injuns hadn't hit us yet, but we knew they was out there. We come out of that canyon, and it looked like a huge dust storm was coming our way, almost like a Kansas tornado—I'm a Missouri kid. Ain't seen nothing like that under a sunny sky before."

"So you didn't see the Apache?"

"No, sir. But the colonel didn't have no doubt. He said there was a lot of the varmints in that dust. He knowed you had a troop up this way and sent me for help, while he led the others back into the canyon. Said they could fort up in the rocks at the dead-end. He didn't think it likely the Apache would attack after dark."

"So you've been out ten hours or more?"

"Yes, sir. Dark slows you down enough, but early on I'd have to slip by Apache and sometimes hide out a spell while they rode past. And like I said, I got lost. Should take half that time, maybe less, in daylight."

Grierson was an odd duck, Flipper thought. The man prided himself on mixing with his troops and did not often direct operations from a fort miles away from combat. He was not inclined to lead wild charges against the enemy, but he tended to be within an easy ride from the action. Regardless, Flipper needed to bring his detachment to the colonel's aid.

"Private, water your horse. Then choose one of the spare mounts and get saddled." In less than twenty minutes, his small troop rode out behind Flipper, whose big sorrel gelding galloped side by side with Private Swenson's bay.

Flipper tried to maintain a steady pace without pushing the horses, and he grudgingly gave soldiers and horses more rest than he liked. But he wanted to arrive at their destination without losing horses or exhausted soldiers. The terrain was rugged, sandy and rocky with many hillocks, ravines and small canyons, but midafternoon, slightly over four hours after Swenson had appeared, he heard the unmistakable cracking of gunfire. He signaled the soldiers to a halt.

They were no more than a hundred yards from the canyon opening and within sight of the Apache attackers if the warriors had not been so focused on the defending soldiers. Flipper pulled his telescope from his saddle bags and studied the scene with a surveyor's eye. He recognized the canyon as a place called Eagle Springs, where he had stopped to water mounts before. He remembered the walls as being high, but the rim to the canyon floor would be well within a rifleman's range. "How deep do you think that canyon is from the rim of the canyon to the floor below?" he asked the private.

"Ain't much good guessing distances, sir, but I'd say seventy-five or eighty feet. Steep as blazes. Nobody's climbing out or in from that end."

"Richards, Moore, and Parker," he hollered. "I've got work for you."

Three cavalrymen pulled out of the column and nudged their mounts forward. All three were sharpshooters and had seen sniper duty with the Union Army during the War of the Rebellion. Richards, currently a corporal after a recent demotion from sergeant following a barroom brawl, was a big man, several inches taller than Flipper and a hundred pounds heavier, darker skinned than the other two who were smaller men.

Flipper said, "I want the three of you to head up to the canyon rim and find yourselves good sniping positions. When you see the rest of us break through the canyon's mouth, start picking targets and drop as many as you can. It will take them a spell to figure out where the rain of lead is coming from."

"Yes, sir," they said in unison. Flipper could see the eagerness in Richards's eyes. He loved this kind of work, and he was the best. Perhaps with success here, he could help boost the man to sergeant's pay again.

Flipper waved the remaining soldiers behind a spiny ridge, where they waited for the snipers to get in place. He pressed his spyglass to his eye and followed his snipers, afoot now, moving up the backside of the canyon towards the rim. When the shooters were positioned, he ordered the men to saddle and follow.

"You had best use your sidearms. Shooting rifles from a saddle tends to be cumbersome and inaccurate. Use your rifles as clubs if it suits you. We will ride two by two, and you will follow me directly through the center of the fighting. Right column, take down the Indians to your right, left to left. That way you won't be shooting each other. Fire when I raise my saber and ride into the enemy. We will try to make our way to the defenders and join them, but I'm hoping to have the devils retreating by then."

Chapter 2
Eagle Springs Attack

FLIPPER, WITH TWO short columns following, reined in his sorrel, pulled out his spyglass, and tried to assess the situation in the dust-clouded canyon. Because of the veil of dust, even with the telescope, he could barely make out the besieged soldiers at the far end of the canyon, perhaps a hundred yards distant. The sporadic gunfire, however, told him that the defense of the rock-strewn fortress on higher ground was near collapse.

The Apache attackers' apparent shortage of rifles had likely been all that allowed Colonel Grierson's party to hold out this long. But now the Apache were closing in like a swarm of bees and would soon overrun the soldiers.

He raised his saber and nudged his mount ahead at a gallop, his colored troopers and Private Swenson following.

Even before they struck the mass of Apache warriors, his snipers started firing from the rim, dropping warriors with deadly accuracy. The rain of lead from above obviously befuddled the targets, as fighters began to tumble from their horses, and they turned away from their objective to locate the source of the gunfire. Then Flipper and his Buffalo Soldiers charged into the melee, Flipper ducking away from the point of a lance and driving his blade into the belly of a fierce-looking, painted warrior. He yanked his weapon free before the warrior could carry it with him as he fell beneath the hooves of the combatants' mounts.

He swung his mount away just as another Apache with warclub raised came for him. He whipped the blade again, slicing deeply into the warrior's neck just short of decapitating him. The sword was not his favorite weapon, and he sheathed the bloody blade in its scabbard and drew his Army Colt from its holster. A pistol shot cracked to his left, and he was nearly jolted from his saddle when an Apache warrior's body fell against his shoulder and slid off the horse's hip to the ground.

He twisted in his saddle to figure out what had happened and saw a grinning Private Swenson astride his mount, Army Colt in hand. "Devil was looking to take your scalp, Lieutenant. Slug in the head put a stop to it."

Flipper said, "I thank you, Private. I'm not quite ready to give it up. I'll see that you get a commendation."

"Don't matter none but glad to have been of service. I think we got them S.O.B.s on the run now."

Flipper sought out his men through the dust curtain that entombed them. Good. They were holding to the ragged double column. Two appeared wounded but were holding onto their horses' reins and still firing. The Apache were yielding space now, trying to slip away into the dust as they retreated to the canyon's mouth.

It appeared that the war party had abandoned any notion of swarming the colonel and his troopers. Private Swenson, a young man he was getting to be quite fond of, was still nearby awaiting orders. "Private, why don't you take me to see the colonel?"

"I'd be proud to do that, sir."

Flipper spoke to his first sergeant, who was not more than five paces away. "Sergeant Miller, I would like you to account for our wounded and see that they are assisted to the colonel's location. I don't think we have any dead, but if so, retrieve the bodies. I would like a count of the Apache dead and wounded."

"Do we kill the wounded, sir?"

"No, not unless the colonel orders it. I understand that the Apache generally return for their dead and wounded, and I suspect we will not be here long."

Chapter 3
Colonel Grierson

FLIPPER DISMOUNTED WHEN he approached Colonel Grierson, a man of average size with a neatly trimmed dark beard, who stood erect with hands clasped behind his back waiting to greet him. Flipper stepped past the bodies of several Apache warriors as he led his horse toward the colonel who waited just in front of the stone-strewed rise.

He noted that the ambulance lay on its side at the base, probably pushed over by the soldiers to provide an extra barrier to ward off Apache arrows. Off to the colonel's left, Flipper saw Sergeant Milo Murphy who tossed him a casual salute when he dismounted. The perpetual smile was fixed on the stocky soldier's light brown face, and Flipper always found Murph's presence buoyed his spirits.

He strode up to the colonel, stood at attention and saluted. "Lieutenant Flipper reporting, sir."

The colonel returned a quick salute and stepped forward and extended his hand. Flipper shifted his gelding's reins to his left hand and shared a firm grip.

"Lieutenant, I must say we're mighty glad to see you. I'm not sure we could have held those Apache off another half hour. With those snipers set up on the ridge and the two-column charge, you caught them by surprise."

"Thank you, sir." The colonel had a reputation as a kind and generous man who had requested that the Ninth and Tenth Cavalry Buffalo Soldiers be included in his command. Flipper had come to admire Grierson as much for his character as for his military strategical skills.

"The soldiers from your troop who made it in with your Sergeant Murphy during the night were a welcome sight. I'm sorry to tell you that two of your young men died during the attack. I believe another was wounded but not seriously. We fortunately have the services of a fine medic who has recruited a few assistants and is tending to the wounded. We lost two others, one from the Ninth. We had six men from the Ninth's Company K slip in last night, too. There was a second lieutenant with them, a classmate and friend of yours, as I recall."

"Jordy?"

"Yes. Lieutenant Jordan Dixon. He's collecting men to right the ambulance at this moment. You will come across him shortly, I'm sure."

"I have ordered my soldiers to take a count of the Apache dead. They may come across a few wounded. I instructed them to do no harm pending further orders."

"A good decision. When our folks are tended to, I will have our medic look at the warriors, if any, and see if he can render temporary aid. I suspect others will return to recover dead and wounded after dusk. We'll post sentries, but I anticipate no more trouble. I think you took the fight out of them. We must always be prepared, of course."

"Is there anything I can assist with now, Colonel?"

"Find your friend, Lieutenant Dixon. Take whatever men you need and tend to the proper burial of our dead. There are many dead horses, but I think my mules survived. Take inventory and capture some Indian ponies to supplement our herd. Secure our camp. It is too late to pull out, and there is much work to be done first. You have authority to commandeer any available soldiers. I will see to getting cooks to work and reorganizing the camp and ambulance. You will find me here."

"Yes, sir. I will do that." He would certainly try.

The colonel looked at him a moment as if evaluating a fine stallion. "You'll do, Lieutenant. My thanks again."

Chapter 4
Old Friends

WHEN COLONEL GRIERSON turned away, Flipper walked over to Sergeant Milo Murphy who had been waiting at a respectable distance. The sergeant came to attention and saluted. Flipper returned the salute, "At ease. I'm glad to see you made it through the Apache to help the colonel, Sarge. The courier told me he came across you."

"Yes, sir. It was middle of the night, and I think the warriors got some spirits someplace and got liquored up some. Anyhow, we led our mounts a good distance and moving slow-like, pretty much walked right into the canyon like we was on a social call. Colonel was dang glad to welcome us that's for sure."

"Well, they needed you, and I doubt if getting in here was as easy as you make it sound. Anyway, we've got work to do. First, I would like you to recruit some men for a burial detail. Collect the bodies, dig separate side by side graves. If you like, I can say some last words when everything's ready."

"Yes, sir. Lonesome place to leave these soldiers."

"We're days from the military cemetery at Fort Davis. No choice. Death is a path we travel alone no matter when and where the end comes."

"I'll think on that, but I don't figure them words will cheer me up none." Murphy turned and headed toward a cluster of malingerers who were not making any efforts to volunteer with tasks. He would remedy that quickly.

Flipper tossed a glance over his shoulder when he heard the crunch of the ambulance wagon wheels hit the rocky ground and the banging and rattling of its contents. The wagon was upright now, and a seasoned colored sergeant who evidently boasted wheelwrighting skills was already under the wagon examining the frame and checking the wheels.

Then he saw Jordan Dixon standing beside the wagon and hurried over to join him. "Jordy," he hollered as he approached.

Jordy swung around, surrendered his crooked grin and stepped toward Flipper, his hand extended. They shared a crunching handshake before embracing briefly and stepping back.

"Dang it, Flip. This is a hell of a way for us to meet up. I can't even take you down the street to a saloon to share a drink."

"You're drinking sarsaparilla these days?"

"You know what I mean. I'll have a frosty beer, and you can drink whatever colored water suits you. We just need to talk."

"I don't know that we'll have much time to catch up today. Your last letter said you would be with the Ninth at Fort Concho. I was with the Tenth at Fort Sill, but when we got orders to head south to Davis, I'd hoped we might stop at Concho. The company commander chose to bypass for some reason."

"Well, my troop and several others from the Ninth are assigned to Fort Davis for temporary duty."

Flipper welcomed that news. He had few close friends, and Jordy topped the list. He was Flipper's age, barely a six-footer with rust-brown hair. He had added a heavy mustache above his lips since their last meeting that made him appear a bit older. That would take some getting used to. "Well, it's good to see you again, Jordy. The general assigned me to some tasks, and I've got to round up the soldiers I rode in with. Maybe we can talk some more later."

"I'm betting we won't get much chance to talk tonight, but I guarantee I'll be clinging like a leech when we get back to Davis. I just want to thank you for saving my scalp today."

"I just showed up with a troop of good soldiers who did their duty."

"Won't argue with you. I learned that back at the Point. But our ledger is out of balance, and I'm on the short end."

"There's no ledger between friends, Jordy."

"I don't care. Sometime I'll find a way to even things up."

Chapter 5
Jordy

WRITERS SAY THAT every person lives a good book if they just took the time to write it. Well, I suppose that's true enough, but some live better books than others. And Henry Ossian Flipper wrote books about his own life, including *The Colored Cadet at West Point and Black Frontiersman: The Memoirs of Henry O. Flipper.*

But some folks live a story at least part of which should be told through the eyes of someone else, and I have taken it upon myself to be that someone. I did not travel with Henry Flipper through childhood, and there were many occasions when we were separated. I learned some about him by way of stories from others, and upon rare occasions he would loosen his own tongue a mite.

Henry was born a slave but emerged, thanks largely to his parents, as a man of keen intellect, coupled with an indomitable spirit that could not be broken. At least he never showed much sign of it during the years we spent together.

Some called Henry, or "Flip" as I tagged him, a loner, and I suppose that was true enough. I dare to lay claim to being his friend, and not many could say that. We shared a good number of adventures in our younger years, some of which I will pass along on these pages. Some of his story, of course, took place before our first meeting, and those I have largely reconstructed from his family and those who knew him in those days and maybe a bit of imagination from time to time. It would have been like pulling teeth to dig some things out of Flip, especially about the ladies he encountered.

For whatever reason, he built fences around some chapters of his life. I confess that I have been known to embellish. I cultivated a certain skill in that direction while writing dime novels and other such fiction, nothing like the intellectual stuff Henry would write.

I met Henry when we disembarked from separate ferry boats on the Hudson River to step onto the grounds at West Point the same day, and how we paired up remains a mystery to me. He was noticed by everybody for sure as the only colored man on the grounds and standing nearly six feet, two inches. He was famous as one of the few colored cadets to ever be admitted, and I had read about him in the newspapers. I understand some Southern publications were outraged at his appointment.

He was a handsome devil, slim and sinewy, and I would have called him a mulatto for his light coppery-hued skin. I later learned that was how he described himself. He told me that he carried some European and Cherokee blood in his veins along with the African. In Louisiana during those years, the state had a complicated system of classifying such things, which always seemed rather silly to me. If I had my way, I would do away with racial classifications. We're mostly a bunch of mongrels anyhow.

I was a Kansas boy from the southwestern most corner of the state, just a few steps from Colorado to the west and Indian Territory, later Oklahoma, to the south. I was raised among ranching and farming people and was a reluctant West Point applicant. There were no colored residents in our county, if you don't count a few Indians. Many of the men, including my father, had fought in the Union Army, and he rose to the rank of brevet colonel during the war, which somehow convinced him that his eldest son should attend the military academy and become an officer. Thus, I was there that day living my father's dream.

Henry, though, was in pursuit of his own dream. Born in Thomasville, Georgia on March 21, 1856, he grew up among a mix of whites and Negroes in a society ruled by whites, even after the war's end. But somehow, he never accepted the notion of his supposed inferiority, in part I suspect because he was raised by parents who disregarded any notions of colored incapability.

That first morning off the boat I happened to fall in line at one of the receiving tables behind Henry Flipper. It only occurred to me later that others were avoiding that line. He moved onto a stool in front of a uniformed sergeant who was asking questions, shuffling papers and pushing them to Henry to sign.

When they were finished, Henry stood, picked up his gear, and stepped away from the stool to make room for me. He looked at me and nodded, giving a small, tight-lipped smile. I extended my hand, and he hesitated, briefly seeming confused. "Howdy," I said. "I'm Jordan Dixon. Call me Jordy."

"Uh, I'm Henry Flipper. Pleased to meet you." He accepted my hand and, at first, I feared his grip had broken a few fingers.

"Next man up. No time to socialize today." It was the sergeant, impatient with my dallying. I would deal with a lot of that in the months ahead.

"I'll likely be seeing you around," I told Henry, who seemed to still be off balance about my greeting. I had no notion at the time that we would eventually be room-mates.

Chapter 6
Thomasville, Georgia

FESTUS FLIPPER WAS nervous about broaching the subject he was on his way to approach his owner, Ephraim Ponder, about. He did not fear Ponder for he was generally a kind and fair man, but he was uncertain how the businessman would take his proposal. Festus considered himself a lucky man when Ephraim purchased him from his late uncle James Ponder's estate for nearly $1,200 several years earlier.

Ponder resided in a mansion in Thomasville, Georgia, a town populated by less than 2,000 people and the county seat of Thomas County with a population of slightly over 10,000 people, of which more than 6,000 were slaves owned by only about ten percent of the white population. He owned farm properties but engaged in assorted business enterprises and was sometimes a financier for others until personal money problems forced him out. Slaves were more an investment than anything else, selling for considerably more than fine horses, and he maintained unusually specious slave quarters and considered it good business to feed and care for his slaves well.

Ponder claimed to be opposed to slavery, but he saw emancipation as some years away until he began to realize the reality of war between the North and South. Festus was grateful that Ponder prepared most of his slaves for freedom and gave them unusual opportunities. He had for half a dozen years or more apprenticed slaves to businesses and manufacturers, sending Festus to Virginia to learn carriage repair and leather crafting, enabling the slave to repair and make shoes, harnesses, saddles and the like.

The owner constructed a large building on his property, where slaves could establish shops to utilize their skills for profit. Slave tradesmen charged local people for their services and even shipped some products to Atlanta. They were allowed to keep their profits after paying Ponder a commission that might vary from ten percent to thirty percent of the net income.

Festus's leather skills were in high demand, and soon he was repairing and making shoes and prospering. He could not read or write since the education of slaves was forbidden by law, but he had an innate understanding of money. He had learned quickly that if folks wanted a new pair of shoes or a saddle repaired, they did not care about the skin color of the person performing the task; they wanted quality work done. A man of any color who could provide a useful skill enjoyed an edge over those who did not.

As was expected, Festus tapped on the back door and waited till it was opened by Maud, one of the house slaves. She was a hefty woman who was the unofficial overseer of the mansion servants and unintimidated by anyone, including her master. She was a dark-skinned woman who had been through tougher times with previous owners than Festus could imagine, so he cut her plenty of slack. How could she have endured all three of her not yet grown children being sold by their master and sent away, never to be seen by their mother again?

"What do you want?" Maud asked.

"Mister Ponder said I could come up and talk with him about something when I got me some time."

"So you think you can just walk in here whenever it suits you?"

"No, I ain't thinking no such thing. Mister Ponder didn't want me to leave until I'd finished fixing a harness.

I seen him when he come down to the shop, and I said I'd like to talk to him private-like."

"Why would he talk to the likes of you in his office?"

Festus tried to be patient. He was only twenty-six years old, and she was twice his age and size. Well, he was taller, but he supposed most would call him skinny despite the sinewy, muscular frame that carried him. "I can't say. You just go and tell Mister Ponder I'm here. If he don't want to see me, I'll go back to the shop."

She slammed the door and left him standing on the step. A few minutes later, she returned and with a disgusted look on her face signaled for him to enter. He followed her in silence through the kitchen and into the beautiful, expansive parlor where she pointed to the office door just off the front entryway.

Festus entered the office where Ephraim Ponder was seated at a mammoth desk surrounded by floor to ceiling bookshelves filled with books that were meaningless to the illiterate man. Ponder, a middle-aged, sturdy man with salt and pepper hair looked up and smiled. "Festus, come in. Sit down, if you like."

Festus remained standing, uncomfortable with the notion of sitting at his owner's desk. "Word is you are moving us all to Atlanta, Mister Ponder, sir."

"Yes, and I can guess why you're here. You don't want to leave your wife, Isabella, and the two boys behind."

"No, sir. I do not. My heart hurts at the notion of leaving Isabella, Henry, and Joseph behind." Henry was three years old now, and Joseph was a newborn.

"I anticipated this, Festus, and I have spoken to their owner, Reverend Luckey. He is sympathetic, but Isabella is very special to their household. He will not let her go without excessive payment, and then the boys have market value also. He demands twenty-eight hundred dollars for the three."

"And you won't pay that."

"I can't. I don't have the money now. Everything I have is being spent on the house and slave quarters I am building on the twenty-five acres near Atlanta. I have borrowed from the banks to do this and will be forced to sell some of my slave properties—not you, of course. You will do very well with your skills in Atlanta and mulattos with your light coloring are especially in demand, however unfair that may be."

"Mister Ponder, I would like to buy my wife and children."

"You have that much money?"

"I do and a bit more. I put all my share of earnings away."

"But you cannot own slaves. You are not a free man, and I cannot yet grant you your freedom."

"I will loan you the money, sir. I'm asking if you might buy Isabella and the boys. I don't care if I ever get paid back. I just want my family with me."

"A strange proposition, Festus. I must think a day or two on this and speak again with Reverend Luckey. I must discuss this with my wife Ellen since Isabella would be a house servant. You go on about your business, and you will hear from me."

As Festus walked back to his shop, he fretted about Ephraim Ponder's discussion with his wife. He did not know the young woman who had married his owner only a few years earlier. He had seen her, of course, and could attest that she was a stunning creature. It was said that she was some fifteen years younger than Mister Ponder and came from a monied family. It was also rumored that she went beyond mere flirtation with other men for occasional pleasures. Such speculation flowed easily among the slave quarters, however, and he would not judge.

He decided he would wait this out, but he would not give up his family. Festus Flipper was nothing if not persistent.

Chapter 7
Atlanta, Georgia

THE FORMER ISABELLA Buckhalter could not believe her good fortune. Her family was truly together for the first time, sharing a separate large room in the new slave quarters on the Atlanta estate. She worked in the two-story stone mansion, spending much of her time in the huge kitchen at the rear. She loved cooking and enjoyed pleasing Miss Ellen who turned out to be a kind and generous mistress.

Isabella loved it here with her family, although Reverend Lucky had always treated her well. Her maiden name was that of her first owner, a man of German heritage, which was common practice among the slaves. At age thirteen, prior to her sale to Reverend Reuben Luckey and his wife, she had been told by her sister, Hagar, that the three sisters were fathered by someone in the Buckhalter family, but she had never confronted her mother about it. She did not care but supposed that would account for her lighter skin color. Slave ancestry was complicated and often uncertain, and she had learned not to dwell upon things that could not be changed.

She had never been mistreated by the Buckhalter family, and Reverend Lucky, a Methodist minister, and his wife had always been kind, even helpful with facilitating her marriage to Festus and arranging a private area in slave quarters for them to spend time together. Of course, they generally had no more than three slaves, which simplified things.

Moreover, Missus Lucky had violated the law by spending hours teaching her to read and write. She had especially taken a liking to numbers and vowed that she would begin teaching Henry soon. Slaves or not, her children would be educated.

Isabella was a willowy woman who after two children would still catch the eye of most men. She loved and respected her husband and thought Festus the handsomest man in Atlanta. She looked to the future without fear and with unbridled optimism. She and Festus hoped for more children, and they would prepare them for life and a freedom that she felt with certainty was on its way.

She was in the kitchen now, assisted by May, a petite girl of sixteen whose help and company she enjoyed. The young woman was a good worker, and together the baked goods they could produce were far more than the household needed. Isabella had a proposal she intended to make to Mister Ponder the next time he was back from Thomasville. She felt it would be of mutual benefit to the Flipper and Ponder families, but she was uncertain of how to broach it. She thought she would discuss it with Missus Ponder first. She would not wish to propose anything that would upset her.

As if on cue, Ellen Ponder walked into the kitchen. "Isabella. May. I wish to speak with you about some changes in the household."

Isabella's heart raced. Were some of the slaves going to be sold? Would her family be split up? She turned away from the stove and faced the mistress, May clutching her arm.

Ellen must have noticed their apprehension. "This is nothing for you to worry about, girls. Ephraim and I will be divorcing, and we are making certain agreements. We have arrived at terms for the Atlanta properties." She held up a sheet of parchment. "This was delivered to me from my husband in Thomasville today." She held up the document to read. "He agrees to indenture all his slaves, men, women and children of various darkness and complexion to me. Do you know what that means?"

Isabella said, "I am not certain."

"You now answer solely to me. I can do anything but sell you or free you without Ephraim and I both approving. The likelihood of both of us agreeing to sale would be very remote. I will now collect all commissions from the workers and craftsmen currently residing at the Atlanta property."

While Ephraim Ponder had always treated them well, Isabella saw the news as a positive development, one that could simplify her plan approval. And Ellen Ponder would give her a free hand in operating her enterprise. Beyond her commissions, she would have no interest in details concerning business operation. "Missus Ponder, I am wondering if we might discuss a business proposition?"

"Well, I don't see why not. What do you have in mind?"

"You have a wonderful kitchen in this house, and I would like to use it for a bakery business. I have discovered a bakery shop in Atlanta that does not have a kitchen one-third this size and simply cannot make enough pastries, bread and such to meet the demand of its customers. The man says he could sell two or three times the products if he had them. I would find out what he needs each day, and May and I could do the baking here and deliver the baked goods to his shop in Festus's buckboard."

"What about your household duties?"

"May and I would continue preparing the meals, but some of the other household servants might need to tend to other chores. There is ample help here."

"That's true enough. We are overstaffed."

"I would pay all costs, including compensation for May and the flour, sugar, fruits and such. I keep books for Festus and will show you a written account of profits each month and pay you thirty percent as your commission."

"I would be willing to try this for three months and see how it works out. If there is a decent commission, and the activity does not upset the peace of the household, I see no reason you could not do this."

"Oh, thank you, ma'am. You won't be sorry. I promise." She would make this enterprise work. She had already discussed the plan with Festus, and he assured her of his support. They would be ready when freedom came, and their family would not starve.

Chapter 8
The War

H ENRY WAS FIVE years old when the South seceded from the United States and triggered a bloody war. During the first few years, Atlanta was a hub of Southern military activity, but the devastation brought by war did not impact the city, and the Flipper family was largely unaffected.

The only battle they witnessed was the war that ignited in 1861, that same year when Ephraim Ponder formally filed for divorce against Ellen on grounds of multiple acts of adultery, among many other misdeeds. The proceedings would go on for ten years, and Ephraim retreated to Thomasville leaving Ellen in sole command at the Atlanta mansion.

Ellen had little day-to-day interest in the activities of the slaves and near total disregard for societal rules or laws and did not object when Isabella prevailed upon a literate slave wheelwright to open a school in his shop evenings. John Quarles was paid a modest sum to educate a small group of slave children, including Henry and, a few years later, Joseph. Henry took to reading, writing, and arithmetic like a fish to water. Quarles later attended law school in the North and eventually became the first Negro to be admitted to the bar to practice law in the state of Georgia.

President Abraham Lincoln's Emancipation Proclamation was issued January 1, 1863, ostensibly freeing all slaves. It had little impact on slaves in the deep South who dared not journey northward at this time. They resided in the Confederate States of America, and the governing officials considered a proclamation by Lincoln meaningless there. But word soon spread through the slave quarters, triggering both jubilation and anguish there.

Freedom was likely on its way, but what then? How did colored folks find food to eat or a roof over their heads when the day of separation from their masters came? Free men and women would become responsible for their own survival and there were frightening aspects of that new reality.

In early 1864 the Ponders were informed that the Confederate Army would be moving into the mansion, the stone structure being one of the sturdiest residences in Atlanta and directly on the path the Union General William Tecumseh Sherman's Army would be taking on its march to attack Atlanta. There was near panic in the city, and civilians were fleeing now. The Ponders, still not quite ready to release their slaves, sent them by rail to Macon to shelter in cellars till the worst of the fighting was over.

It was a miserable time for Festus, Isabella, and their two young sons. Food rations were scarce, and the war's outcome was obviously rendering the so-called Confederate "greybacks" worthless. Isabella had stashed Union gold coins whenever she or Festus collected the money surreptitiously for their services. This would be their capital when the war ended. She carried a small bagful in her satchel but dared not use the coins that might invite theft or confiscation by Confederate soldiers.

When Atlanta fell and was virtually destroyed by Sherman's troops, the Flippers returned to Atlanta to find a battered Ponder mansion that had been gutted by fire. It was uninhabitable, as were the slave quarters. Festus and Isabella, with little Henry, built a temporary lean-to shelter from scrap lumber on the property where they lived for several months.

Later they located an intact house and purchased that for the family and for a bakery Isabella was determined to establish. Nearby was a brick-fronted store building that they purchased for Festus's shoe and leather business.

Soon Isabella was cooking for Union officers and, with the assistance of May and several other former household servants, selling baked goods to the public as well as Union soldiers. Festus was nearly overwhelmed with shoe repairs and orders for custom-made boots and shoes. Now they were paid in Union Currency that was spendable throughout the town. Henry was put to work in the shop at age ten, but a Confederate widow was employed to continue with the education of the boys.

For the remainder of his lifetime, Henry recalled the return to Atlanta and the sight of lynched Confederate soldiers hanging from trees and rotting corpses cluttering the lawns. The only effort at burial appeared to consist of tossing a few shovelfuls of dirt or sand over the dead soldiers, leaving much of their bodies exposed. Months later, some were identified and families notified to retrieve the remains. Those not claimed were loaded into wagons and hauled away to be buried in common graves.

Isabella and Festus welcomed another child, Festus Jr., in 1868. About this time the American Missionary Association established a school in Atlanta. The teachers were primarily from the North and not warmly received by residents, but the Flippers promptly saw that their sons were enrolled. The school's facilities were at first established in an old church, and then an abandoned railroad car was added, before several houses were added, and finally a new building. The American Missionary school is where Henry fine-tuned his education before he enrolled at Atlanta University in 1872.

Chapter 9
The Aspiring Cadet

URING HIS FIRST year at Atlanta University, Henry decided that he would like to attend the military academy at West Point. He had read of the superior education offered there at no cost but a commitment to serve in the Army as a commissioned officer for eight years. He would become a second lieutenant upon graduation and, moreover, a qualified engineer.

He could not explain why the notion had grabbed him so firmly, but he had been impressed with the officers he encountered when helping his mother serve meals at their home or when he helped her deliver meals to their quarters. They had unfailingly treated him and his family with kindness and respect, often not the case with Atlanta natives following the war. Besides, his mother was with child again, and it was time to venture out on his own.

The key to attending West Point was newly elected congressman James C. Freeman, a radical Republican. The Republicans held a near monopoly on Southern elected officials during the years immediately follow-ing the war. The Reconstruction Act enacted by Congress temporarily suspended voting rights of public officials serving during the conflict and former Confederate of-ficers, and colored males were assured the right to vote at this time.

Thus, for a brief time, the Republicans dominated the representation in Congress. Congressman Freeman, rep-resentative from Georgia's Fifth District, had the power to nominate candidates for appointment to West Point, and Henry prepared and sent him an application together with physical examination forms, school transcripts, and letters from teachers and others. After several months, he received a reply acknowledging that his application had been received and inviting him to Augusta for an in-terview with Congressman Freeman.

Henry was nervous that day when he was scheduled to meet the Republican congressman at his Augusta office. This was not a common experience for the seventeen-year-old, whose parents occasionally called him "Unbroken," comparing him to a horse that stubbornly refused to surrender its independence and submit easily to reins and saddle. Opinions of others mattered little to him, and he simply ignored those who tried to demean him or block him from whatever goal he was attempting to achieve at a given time.

But one man stood in his way today, and although he did not doubt his ability to meet the challenges of West Point and ultimately graduate and be commissioned a second lieutenant, there was a single man with the power to stop him dead in his tracks.

When he embarked from the train, satchel in hand, Henry walked directly to Congressman Freeman's office, having obtained the address and researched the location earlier. It was no more than six blocks from the station. It was shortly after one o'clock and his appointment was not till three. He had taken an early train because train schedules were unreliable, and he did not want to risk tardiness and decided that he would check in at the congressman's office to make the representative aware that he had arrived and was available.

He was surprised when he arrived at the office address and found that Representative Freeman headquartered in a small clapboard house with peeling whitewash.

The congressman's offices were obviously not a strain on the federal budget.

He entered the office and was greeted by a young colored woman at a single, scarred and scratched desk. She looked up at Henry and captured him with a welcoming smile. "I am Rose Hawthorn, and I am guessing you are Mister Henry Ossian Flipper."

She took him by surprise with both her recognition of him and beauty that could not be subdued by the blue business skirt and jacket she wore. "Yes, ma'am. I am a couple hours early. I just got off the train and thought I would check in to assure the congressman that I will be here on time. Then I will try to find a night's lodging place and a meal before I return."

She picked up a piece of paper from her desk and stood. She was a tall, lithe woman and stepped toward him with a handwritten note. "I suspected you might need this. A very nice boarding house serving evening meals and breakfast. Available to colored folks. Anyone is welcome, but I've never seen a white person there in the year I've lived in the house. There are close to a dozen rooms, and there are almost always vacancies."

"That's good. I don't want to run into trouble."

"Maribelle—she's the landlady—will ask you if you've had anything for lunch, and I'm betting she'll have a beef sandwich and piece of apple pie for you. If not, there's a small café across the street. I've written down the names and addresses of both places."

"You are very well organized. This had been a worry. Thank you."

"You are very welcome. That's what I am paid to do. Congressman Freeman wishes me to make folks feel welcome here. This is the first job I've held with a fancy title. 'Assistant' of all things. Of course, I am the only employee, so I also clean, and on Saturdays, scrub floors." She gave a soft laugh. "Now, you go and get back early, so I can tell you a few things about the congressman before you meet with him. 'Belle's Bed and Board' is just two blocks north and off on a side street a bit. You can't miss it."

"Yes, ma'am. Thank you, ma'am."

"Rose. Please call me Rose."

A half hour later, after settling in a pleasant, immaculate room at Belle's Bed and Board, Henry sat at the kitchen table with Mirabelle Duncan, the proprietor, who, per Rose's prediction had just served up a delicious roast beef sandwich and a cup of hot coffee. A scrumptious-looking slice of apple pie awaited his attention.

Mirabelle, an attractive full-figured woman in her late forties, Henry guessed, sat down across from him, studying the young guest who had been sent to her boarding house by Rose. She seemed to have a perpetual smile pasted on her mahogany-colored face, even when her dark eyes betrayed concern, or now, curiosity.

They exchanged small talk, not revealing much personal information. Finally, she moved to satisfy her curiosity. "Y'all said you come all the way from Atlanta by train? Ain't never been to Atlanta. Hope y'all don't mind my saying so, but you sound like an educated young man."

"Well, I finished high school and just started college."

"I can read and write some but none too good. Ain't had no formal schooling. Know my numbers good, though. I can add the customer's bill up just fine. You're a lucky youngster. Y'all can go places."

"Lucky to have parents who insisted on my getting an education and that freedom came at the right time for me to do that."

"Rose is educated, but I'm sure she has told you all about that. Of course she comes from up north. Pennsylvania, she calls it. Took me forever to learn that word. Ya'll heard of that place?"

"Yes, ma'am, but I have never been there. That's where the Battle of Gettysburg was fought."

"That I heard of. You and Rose been friends for a long time?"

"No, ma'am. Our first meeting was in the congressman's office this morning. I have an appointment with the congressman this afternoon. She suggested I might put a nice roof over my head and find some fine eating here." He took the last bite of his pie. "She was right about both. I have never eaten a better apple pie."

"Y'all can charm a lady, that's for sure. I figured y'all was Rose's beau from up north. You don't talk Georgian—well, just a hint maybe."

Henry shrugged and smiled. "I'm Georgian and proud to be." His teachers had mostly been from the North, and he had consciously worked to eliminate his accent, so he took her observation as a compliment.

"And y'all are going to meet with Congressman Freeman?"

He decided to halt her fishing venture and told her about his mission in Augusta. "I am not an important visitor, I assure you, but Mister Freeman has been kind enough to interview me."

"A soldier? Going to school to be a soldier. I've heard of this West Point. Many of the Southern generals went there, Lee hisself, I heard."

"That's true, and J.E.B Stuart, Stonewall Jackson, and nearly 150 others. Add President Jefferson Davis to the list."

Chapter 10
The Interview

WHEN HENRY RETURNED to Congressman Freeman's office, about forty-five minutes remained until his scheduled appointment. When he walked into the waiting area, he was instantly warmed by Rose's smile.

"Sit down," she said. "You look well fed. I assume you and Mirabelle struck it off just fine."

He claimed a chair directly in front of her desk. "Oh, yes. A very nice room, and I was served a huge slice of delicious apple pie, as you predicted. I liked her very much, and I ended up doing most of the talking. She should have been a spy, the way she digs out information. I am not known for loosening my tongue that way."

"Yes, you don't keep many secrets from Mirabelle living at her boarding house, but I adore her. We will be sharing supper there this evening, and I hope you will chat with me afterward. You are very interesting, and I would like to know more about you. But, for now, I want to prepare you for your interview with Congressman Freeman."

"I welcome any help I can get."

"First, you must understand that you are the only colored candidate he will be interviewing. There are at least two others, both sons of wealthy families with political influence, who are successful businessmen that aided the Union during the war but succeeded in continuing their operations quietly in Georgia. There were more of those than you might think. The congressman himself owns vast lands and held slaves that he prepared for freedom and emancipated before the Proclamation. Many remained with him as hired hands and craftsmen."

"I was born as a slave to a father who enjoyed the benefit of such an owner."

"That explains a few things. The thing you must understand is that you will receive no preference because of your race. Congressman Freeman is an honest man. He is a Republican who barely won election because of the new male, colored voters and the fact that former

Confederate officers are by law prohibited from voting. Those restrictions will phase out soon. His hold on his seat is precarious. Selection of a colored nominee will not be popular with many white folks."

"So you are warning me that my color may stop him from appointing me."

"Absolutely not. I just wanted you to know how things are. He must be convinced of your chances of success at the academy, that you are the most qualified selection. He does not want to embarrass you or our race by sending a failure to West Point."

"I do not wish the appointment because of my race. That would be an insult to me and all colored people. I want to be chosen because I am best qualified."

She looked at him a moment, her dark eyes fixed on his. "You truly mean that, don't you?"

"Why should I not? It is foolish and wrong to expect more. I have worked very hard to make a worthy life for myself. If the congressman decides I am not the best to fill the vacancy, then I will move on and be the best at something else."

"I think I was foolish to think I could coach you for your interview. You will do better if you ignore my words. I think you will be fine. I like you, Henry. We must talk more this evening. I want to know more about you."

"And I like you, Rose, and look forward to it."

The door to the congressman's office opened, and a nattily dressed, coat and vested man with a handlebar mustache stepped out, followed by a blond-haired young man about Henry's age, wearing a suit and tie. The sober-faced younger man nodded at Henry, and he returned a feeble wave. The older man, obviously the father, tossed him a hostile look.

After the other visitors departed, Rose got up and entered the congressman's office, pulling the door shut behind her. Henry could hear the low mumble of voices from within and assumed they were speaking about him. It was ten minutes or more before the door opened and Rose appeared.

"Mister Flipper, Congressman Freeman will see you now. Please come in." She gave Henry a smile and a re-assuring nod as she held the door open as he passed through.

As the door closed behind him, Henry found himself enclosed in a small room that must have once served as someone's bedroom. A burly, middle-aged man stepped out from behind the desk with extended hand, a smile half-hidden behind the graying beard that cloaked his face. They shook hands with firm grips, and Freeman stepped back, looking up at the much taller Henry.

"You're a tall young feller, but I guess your doctor's report already told me that. I'm Jim Freeman by the way. Come, sit in front of my desk a spell."

The congressman had a deep voice that reminded him of a bear's growl, but it was a congenial growl. They sat down at the desk facing each other, and Freeman shuffled through a stack of papers on his desk. The silence was starting to make Henry uneasy, when finally, the congressman looked up and spoke. "I got a book collected on you, Mister Flipper, stacked here on my desk. Doctors' reports, school records, letters from teachers and others. Some you sent, but we make independent inquiries, too."

"I understand, sir."

"Do you understand that my submission of your appointment would not guarantee your admission?"

"I do. I would be required to take additional testing at the academy, physical and academic evaluations. There are standards I would be required to satisfy. I am confident I can do that."

"I see. You do realize that there would be no more than one other colored student in the entire cadet corps?"

"Yes, I discovered that in my reading. James Webster Smith is currently enrolled, I believe, although I read he was on probation the last term."

"He has a reputation as a troublemaker and has not been helpful to the cause of colored people in the military. If I should appoint you, many white voters and Southern newspapers are going to raise a racket. I'll be placing my head on the chopping block. I simply do not want you embarrassing me or our district."

"I do not wish to embarrass either you or the district, and most of all I do not desire to embarrass myself. I know the road ahead is not an easy one, but I will satisfy the qualification tests, and I will be a credible representative of the people of Georgia, white and colored."

"You don't lack confidence. I will give you that."

"I was raised to believe in what I can do, sir. I want this appointment but only if I am the most qualified. I ask neither to be granted this honor because of my race nor to be denied because of it."

The congressman stared at him in silence for what seemed like eternity, although Henry knew it was only seconds. Then he sighed. "I will certify your name as my appointee, Mister Flipper. You may inform your parents, but any public announcement will come from my office. I will deny that a decision has been made until the time of my choosing, and you will not receive formal notice till that time. I must decide on the appropriate political timing and way to announce this. Can you understand this?"

Nothing could subdue Henry's exuberance at this moment, but outwardly he appeared calm. "I know nothing about politics, Congressman, but I will say nothing to anyone but my parents. They are very discreet people. I can only thank you for this. I will try to be a credit to your judgment."

Chapter 11
Rose Hawthorn

ROSE WAS ASSISTING a constituent in the outer office when Henry left the congressman's office, so they did not have an opportunity to speak again until they sat across from each other at the supper table. Their conversation was stiff and formal because of the presence of three other guests and Mirabelle Duncan, but Henry enjoyed healthy helpings of baked ham, sweet potatoes, and green beans, topped off, of course, with more of the landlady's apple pie. Most of all, he enjoyed furtively watching the pretty lady sitting across the table.

After supper, the landlady announced, "Rose has asked if she might reserve the parlor this evening to chat with Mister Flipper, and I told her it was available. I hope y'all will respect that."

The announcement caught Henry by surprise, and he froze in his chair for a moment, looking at the other guests out of the corners of his eyes. He relaxed when he saw that the two men appeared disinterested, and the older woman just had a benign smile on her face. As the other guests got up from the table, he looked at Rose, who was also rising.

She looked at him impishly. "Well, are you going to join me in the parlor?"

When they entered the small parlor adjacent to the dining room, Rose took his hand and led him to a leather-cushioned loveseat that showed signs of wear but was quite comfortable. He was still uneasy, uncertain what to say. He could recite algebraic formulas or Shakespearean lines instantly upon request or write countless pages on a myriad of subjects, but he had little experience with girls or women. He knew Rose would be several years older than he was.

Rose was looking at him now, her dark, limpid eyes mesmerizing. "How old are you?" Rose asked.

"Uh, seventeen."

She laughed. "You told the truth. I knew. I saw it on your application. You're a truthteller. I like that. Most young men your age would lie if they were sitting in a loveseat with an older woman. I am twenty-one. Do you find me homely?"

Why was she asking that? "I'm a truthteller. I find you incredibly beautiful."

She reached over and gently caressed his cheek. "Perfect answer. I knew there was a lothario hidden there, just waiting to leap out."

This was starting out as the strangest conversation he had ever had, especially with a female. "I want to thank you for the help you gave me in preparing for the interview."

She moved her hand from his cheek, which had been making him nervous and inciting discomfort in his britches. When her hand dropped away, however, her fingers brushed softly over his crotch. It was likely accidental, but she would have felt the hardness beneath the denim. He was starting to perspire.

"I know you have won the appointment to the academy," she said. "The Congressman told me. It had been mostly decided before your interview. Your credentials were far more impressive than those of the other applicants, but he wanted to meet you to be satisfied you have the toughness and character to persevere. The appointment will be controversial in some quarters. Whatever you said convinced him you could do it."

"I can."

"Tell me, what do you want to do when you graduate?"

"Go west. Serve with the Ninth or Tenth regiments of the Buffalo Soldiers. They are colored soldiers, of course, but they have never been under command of a colored, commissioned officer. I would like to be the first. I will command white soldiers, too, someday, but this would be my start."

"But the west? It is uncivilized out there. Savages to fight. Totally removed from the modern conveniences in the east. I would never go there."

He was disappointed at her lack of adventurous spirit. "I just want to use my education in a new place, help break-in a fresh land. Yes, I will go to the west. It has been calling me since I was a boy."

"Yes. And I have no doubt you will answer that call." She hesitated a moment. "You seem so confident."

"I suppose. About some things."

"Are you a virgin?"

"What?"

"Have you ever been intimate with a girl or woman? I'm trying to put it delicately."

"Should we be talking about such things?" This was getting on scary ground.

"I don't know why not. I am an unmarried woman, and you are a single man. You want me. I felt you. I can sense it." She looked at his crotch before she lifted her head, and their eyes met. "Tell me, truthteller, would I be your first?"

"Uh, yes."

"Then, I want you to join me in my room, and I will teach you things. You will spend most of the night, but I must send you to your room before sunrise."

"But the rules . . ."

"Mirabelle makes exceptions so long as she is informed. She knows. My room is at the end of the hall. No one is lodged adjacent tonight, which pleases me since I am sometimes noisy. I will go to my room now. Give me fifteen minutes, go to the house entryway, take the hallway to your right. Walk to the end of the hall. My name is on the doorframe since I am a full-time resident. Do not rap. Push the door open and walk in. I don't think you will encounter anyone, but if you do, just walk away and try again a bit later."

She got up and disappeared quickly as a spirit. Maybe she was a spirit. This simply could not be happening to him. He was at once excited and fearful, afraid that he would make a fool of himself with his inexperience.

When he crept into Rose's room, he found he need not have worried. School was in session. He disrobed her slowly as she instructed, piece by piece until the perfectly formed creature stood naked beside him. She told him where and why to touch her and then undressed him, albeit faster as if in a hurry. He was too enflamed with lust when she examined him standing in front of her and whispered, "Oh my," to wonder what she meant.

She embraced him and pressed her lips to his for a lingering kiss, and it was almost more than he could bear. "On the bed," she said. "On your back."

Confused, he obeyed, and she was on him instantly like a cat. Soon, he went to heaven, having never known such ecstasy. She moaned and collapsed on top of him. She was breathing hard, and between breaths, she said, "You are young. It would have been torture for you to wait, and I was very—let us say, needy. We are far from finished. I have much to teach you. Before the night is over, you will learn many ways to please a woman, and I daresay you will excel."

The night ended too soon, but he was sated. Still, he did not want to leave her. Was this love? She kissed him one last time before he dressed to go back to his room to capture a few hours' sleep. "When will I see you again?" Henry asked.

"Just remember this night and that I was your first. You leave on a train later this morning for Atlanta. There will be no more for us. I had a memorable night, and I am jealous of the women in your future. But our lives have different destinations, Henry. You know that. We should all be grateful for these moments that we stumble onto. I will think of you fondly from time to time and wish only good things for you."

She rolled over and buried her head in her pillow. Surely, those were not muffled sobs he heard when he slipped out the door. He would never, never forget Rose Hawthorne.

Chapter 12
Jordy

HENRY FLIPPER AND I both passed our qualification tests at West Point, although I have no doubt his scores were higher than mine. He was a master of English grammar and sentence structure and dwarfed my skills at mathematics. I always thought of myself as a competent writer, and, in fact, aspired to be an author of dime novels or a newspaper journalist before I detoured to West Point. But even as I write these words, I am intimidated by the possibility my old friend might read them and start parsing my sentences.

In the early months, Flipper and I were only casual acquaintances, but somehow, we gravitated to each other as the days rolled by. We shared a few of the more academically traditional classes such as Spanish, where he was the top student in the class, as well as geology and chemistry. We often teamed up on military drill and strategies, but the only place where I could flaunt superiority was on horseback where we learned cavalry skills and techniques. He was not raised on horseback as I was, and, although Flipper became a fair horseman, I daresay I could always outride him. Grant me one victory.

I probably became his friend by default. Although he was not hazed more than any other plebe that first year, classmates tended to avoid him in places where others might see. In private some would converse with him and display signs of friendship, but in public they would barely know him. I liked the guy a lot and didn't care what others thought, so I ended up with Flipper in the group situations most of the time. I do not hold myself out as a paragon of kindness and virtue. On the contrary, I can be the worst of assholes on occasion. I just felt comfortable with old Flip, and he helped me with my struggles in engineering and chemistry classes.

Our first year, Flipper roomed with another colored cadet, James Webster Smith, who was the first colored cadet admitted to West Point several years earlier but had been set back a year for disciplinary reasons. Flipper told me he was pleased when he learned Smith would be assigned as his roommate, thinking it would be nice to share a room with another colored student. His first thought turned into a nightmare.

Smith was an intelligent young man but had a fiery temper. He interpreted any slight or traditional hazing as a racial attack and resorted quickly to his fists or refused to obey orders. Flipper tired of the student's rants about inequality. Call Smith "nigger" and he would explode, even though this happened rarely. Flipper came to dislike his roommate intensely. He thought that on occasion Smith might have been disciplined more harshly than a white student, but he was convinced that his roommate could have avoided the problem by focusing on his classwork, which was suffering from occasional incarcerations and lack of attention.

Flipper was relieved when Smith was finally expelled from the academy. He was saddened for the young man, but it was difficult to suffer anyone who might interfere with his own graduation goal. He might endure occasional social stings along his journey, but to him the path to equality was knowledge and personal achievement.

My own roommate failed several classes that first year and dropped out of school, and I immediately volunteered to be Flipper's roommate, which appeared to be a relief to the room coordinator. That is when I really got to know this man. Selfishly, the move also assured me of my own graduation. I was granted a personal tutor who cheerfully coached me through several of my weaker subjects. Sometimes, I was tempted to let fate flunk me out of the place. I was not a motivated student, and my head was often somewhere other than at West Point. Still, I was not raised to be a quitter and did not want to go back to the Kansas ranch with my tail between my legs. I would finish this dang thing.

It must have been tough on Flipper sometimes. For the most part, he was not treated differently than any other cadet, especially in the classroom, and that was all he ever asked. Yet he was never accepted as a part of the corps by most of the other cadets. He was looked upon as something of an oddity and not generally welcomed into the ranks.

After that first year, some students organized to sneak into town at night to party at the taverns and, with luck, find a willing woman. He was never invited, although he likely would have declined. He did not touch spirits, and he would not risk the discipline that might result from an excursion.

I ventured out once for a night of merrymaking. Flipper said nothing, but the guilt of leaving him behind sent me home after one beer. The others got caught when they returned later, so Flipper, without even knowing, saved me from demerits and a few nights in the guardhouse.

Flipper was a solid student through all four years at the academy, excelling especially in Spanish and engineering related subjects, but he would not graduate at the top of his class, more likely closer to the middle. I must confess that I finished in the bottom ten percent but considered myself fortunate to walk away with my commission.

Neither Flipper nor I would look back at our West Point days with nostalgia. My friendships were few outside of Flipper, partially, I suppose, because of my association with him. On the other hand, I am not a social creature and probably do not carry a welcoming demeanor. Flipper never complained, but he had grown up in a protected environment with parents who held him close and white missionary teachers who insulated colored students from racial epithets and bullying.

It did not happen often, but more than once I heard him called "nigger," and I saw older cadets try to goad him into fisticuffs, but he never responded, walked on as if he had not heard the insult or the challenge. Once, he grabbed my arm firmly and led me off when I was readying to intercede. He obviously did not like the risks of blame if he did take the bait and get into a fight. His self-discipline has never been equaled by anyone I encountered.

Graduation day on June 14, 1877, was worth remembering. Speakers included Secretary of War James G. Blaine and Major General Winfield Scott. That day, many classmates who had only furtive contact with Flipper shook his hand and congratulated him. When he walked across the outdoor stage to receive his diploma, the audience and his classmates applauded loudly, and he surrendered one of his rare smiles.

The newspaper folks were there that day also, and the reporting on the first colored graduate dwarfed the paragraphs on the speakers' words. For the most part, the press praised Flipper's accomplishment, however some speculated that he would never be able to command white troops. Others suggested that fellow officers would not welcome him. Some Southern newspapers, but not all, claimed he was a token who had not earned his place in the graduating class.

I doubt if Flipper suspected on graduation day that he would make many more headlines in the newspapers during the years in front of him.

Chapter 13
Atlanta Furlough

ENRY STROLLED WITH Anna White in a park
set aside especially for colored people in Atlanta. While the segregation of such facilities
disappointed him, he saw no point to making a fuss over
such things. In his mind, time would sort this out someday. Regardless, he had no interest in doing anything
that might stand in the way of his military career. He had
worked too hard to arrive at this point.

It was a brisk November day, and he had been on furlough in Atlanta waiting for his commission and Army
assignment. Anna was a striking, poised young woman
attired like a traditional Southern belle who might have
been mistaken for a mistress of a grand plantation home
were it not for her dark, bronze-colored skin.

Anna was twenty-years old and a grade schoolteacher at one of the missionary schools for colored children. Her mother taught also, and her father prospered as the proprietor of a small freight company. Like his own parents, hers had been prepared and undaunted by their new freedom. Sadly, this was not the case for many.

He had met Anna at a church party and been attracted immediately to this intelligent woman. They saw each other frequently over the next several months, usually at her home where they were chaperoned by her parents except when they could escape to the front porch swing on warm evenings and exchange furtive kisses.

They spoke easily with each other, and he had never talked with another woman so much. He shared feelings and experiences with Anna that he had shared with no other person. He had come to love her and asked her to marry him.

At her insistence, he had asked her rather taciturn father for Anna's hand in marriage. He could tell that the somber-faced man consented reluctantly, and the mother's eyes and set chin signaled outright disapproval. But they were engaged now, and Henry had even given her a ring, albeit imitation stone, with a promise that he would do better for her when he had funds. She assured him that his love was enough.

They had never been physically intimate beyond their kisses. Anna, without saying as much, had always made it clear that more affection must wait till marriage. But he wanted her, and he thought she reciprocated desire.

Anna had been uncharacteristically silent during their stroll, but he liked that they could enjoy quiet times together. Still, he sensed that something was bothering her. He nodded toward a bench on the edge of the stone walk. "Something is on your mind. Shall we sit down and talk?"

"Yes. I think we should."

They sat down, and silence still ruled for some moments before Anna spoke. "I hope you haven't purchased an engagement ring yet."

"No, we had agreed to do that together."

"The engagement is over."

He had not been prepared for this. "I don't understand."

"After you told me about your assignment two days ago, I discussed it with my parents. You will be going west for who knows how long. There are still Indian troubles there, and you will be with the Tenth Cavalry. My father has looked into it and says the Buffalo Soldiers are being sent to the worst of that fighting, and you may not be back for several years."

"But the first of January I will receive my commission. I will be an officer, and my wife can join me at my Army posting. I had assumed you would travel there, and we would live in married officer housing. We can be married before I leave or after you arrive at the post. Your choice. You will be safe at the fort."

"But you will be out on missions. You will not be safe."

"We have talked about this, there are risks to being a soldier, but they are not great these days with the Indian wars coming to an end."

"But there are still renegades out there, and the Apache are resisting. That's what my father says."

"We have talked about this for weeks. I thought you had come to terms with it."

"I thought I had, too, but now that reality has arrived, I just cannot do it. My parents are adamantly opposed. I am their only child. They are afraid of losing me, and I realize now that I do not want to go west. I will be alone most of the time in an uncivilized land. If I went, I know I would return home within a month. You would not want that embarrassment."

"Don't think about any embarrassment on my part. And you would not be alone. There would be other wives at the Army post. You would make friends."

"How many of the officers' wives are colored?"

"Well . . . I suppose there would be none."

"I would be alone."

"I know they would welcome you. I am told there is genuine camaraderie among officers' wives. They look after each other."

"You cannot say how they would treat a Negro woman."

"Most would extend a hand of friendship. If colored people are to have good lives, they must get past their own negative expectations. I have refused to accept my color as a cross to bear, and I will not acknowledge my color as a burden. I have found fellow soldiers for the most part welcoming. Some stationed in Atlanta have become quite good friends during my stay here. Sometimes we get what we expect."

"I am afraid, Henry. I just cannot do it. I will not do it. Nothing you can say will change my mind. You have become a dear friend, and I do not want to end that. But unless you can get a change of assignments, I cannot be your wife."

Henry did not have to ponder this. "If I requested a change of assignments, that would be the first nail in the coffin of my Army career. Besides, I got the exact assignment I wanted. I wouldn't ask for a change even if it were possible."

"Then it is over."

"Do you still wish to see me while I am here?"

"I would love that if you will not press me to change my mind."

"I will not, but know that you still have that option."

Chapter 14
The Journey Begins

AFTER RECEIVING HIS second lieutenant's commission on January 2, 1878, Flipper's first destination was by rail to Houston, Texas where he received his official orders from General John W. Davidson. He learned that he was to report to Colonel Benjamin Grierson at Fort Sill, Indian Territory where the Ninth and Tenth Cavalry regiments were being organized.

He hoped to meet up with his academy roommate Jordy Dixon there. Jordy was home at the family ranch in southwest Kansas and had been assigned to the Ninth regiment according to a letter received only a week before his departure from Atlanta. Jordy was still a reluctant soldier, but he would do his duty, and Flipper had missed his company.

He had taken a train from Houston to Fort Worth and now was aboard a stagecoach for a three-day ride to Fort Sill to the northwest. Passengers would be spending two nights at relay stations during the stretch. Two mounted Army privates would accompany the stage which carried a box of gold coins for distribution as a semi-annual allotment to Comanche occupying the reservation adjacent to Fort Sill. Script for purchases at stores on or near the post was also issued quarterly, according to the tall stage driver, a white-haired, bony man called "Red," a nickname Flipper supposed was tagged on in his younger years.

"I'm glad to have me another soldier aboard," Red said, when Flipper appeared at the stage in Fort Worth. "Two men ain't enough to guard this cargo. I don't know what them higher-ups is thinking, but I think they got shit for brains. It's a good bet we got more than thirty thousand dollars in that steel box in the cargo hold."

"Doesn't Wells Fargo provide another guard to ride up front with you?"

"Oh, yeah. I got me a feller riding shotgun—some snot-nosed kid I never rode with before. He'll be coming along in a few minutes, I hope. Them youngsters these days got no sense of being on time. I hope he knows which end of a rifle the slug comes out of." He spat a wad of tobacco, leaving a bit dripping from the droopy mustache that half covered his lips.

Flipper said, "Somebody with a rifle and a bag is trotting this way now."

Red said, "Yep, that's Roddy. The short, skinny kid. Met him over at the station earlier. Think it's his first time on a run."

The young man was nearly out of breath when he reached them. Flipper guessed him to be about twenty years old. He had a narrow, black mustache over thin lips and dark eyes that avoided meeting his own. He seemed edgy and nervous, but that was understandable on his first job.

"Running late," Roddy said.

Red said, "Well, we're moving out. Get your ass and gear up on top."

"Only one other passenger today," Red told Flipper. "Wells Fargo would drop this line if the government didn't contract to keep it going. Sometimes, I get full loads on the return trip. Seems like more leaving than going, which I can't figure."

When Flipper climbed into the coach, he was surprised to see that the other passenger was a woman. He tipped his hat and took a seat on the opposite, rear side of the coach, laying his duffel bag and rifle on the vacant space beside him. His sword was sheathed and tucked in the duffel bag.

"Good morning, Lieutenant," the woman said. "You are Lieutenant Henry Flipper. I am Mollie Dwyer." She was a young woman with dark brown eyes and chestnut-colored hair. She had a glint in her eyes that was more mischievous than flirtatious.

"Uh . . . good morning. How did you know . . ?" He shrugged. "I guess there aren't that many colored lieutenants around."

"I hope I didn't offend you in some way. You are famous, you know. Please call me Mollie. We are going to be seeing a lot of each other the next several days. I hope we can be friends."

"Only if you will call me Henry. Be patient with me. You don't seem to be fearful of my company."

She giggled. "You aren't very intimidating."

They were both shaken for a moment with the jerk of the three teams of horses pulling the stage forward. Flipper said, "I guess our journey has begun. Are you comfortable with your back to the front? We can trade sides."

"Why don't you put your gear over next to my mine, and I will move over to yours?" She smiled. "Don't worry. I'll keep my distance. We can each sit nearer a window."

"If you are comfortable with that."

"Why wouldn't I be?" She moved over to his side and he shifted his rifle and duffel bag to hers.

"There. That didn't hurt, did it? I do think this will be more comfortable, facing the direction we are traveling."

What man would object to a pretty, young lady sharing a seat? He knew many white women, but he had never encountered one who seemed so at ease with a colored man. Or perhaps he, like so many of both white and colored people, was too conscious of color differences.

As they bounced along the rutted trail that was called a road, Mollie Dwyer continued to lead the conversation. "May I ask what your assignment is at Fort Sill?"

"I have been assigned to the Tenth Cavalry. I am to report to a Colonel Grierson."

"Oh, such a coincidence. My brother-in-law, Captain Nicholas Nolan, will be assigned to the Ninth and Tenth regiments. He recently married my sister. He's a handsome devil and very nice. I think he expects some babies from her. He has been a widower for some years and had a boy and a girl with his first wife. Men like lots of babies since they don't do much to see to their care."

"I see." But he did not. This was none of his business.

"Annie insisted that I come live with them. We were living in San Antonio in my parents' old house. My father served as an officer in the Confederate Army, and my older brother died in battle. Father was a lawyer, quite prosperous before the war, but of course Confederate dollars became worthless, and many of his clients were driven to poverty after the war. The Union carpetbaggers moved in and saw that anyone with Confederate ties lost their properties. Father saved the house, but he died a half dozen years ago and mother shortly after. Annie and I both found teaching jobs with a Christian mission school and earned enough to subsist."

"You have not had an easy life then."

"I am not complaining. Please understand that. I am alive and our situation will improve. I hope to teach at one of the Indian schools near Fort Sill. We were about to lose the home to increased taxes that we could not pay, so I see this as a fresh start."

Flipper could not help but like this woman who was talking his ear off. "I'm sure things will work out."

"Your turn."

"What do you mean?"

"I've been telling you the story of my life. Now I want to hear yours."

"You have apparently read mine."

"I've read what others have said about you. Some of the Southern papers have not been kind. But you are famous. I want to hear what this famous person has to say about himself. Why did you end up at West Point?"

"A free education. And then I thought the military might be an interesting and challenging career. I'm fascinated by the structure, and I have ambitions, but I received an education that will open other doors, like engineering, if the Army does not work out. Sometimes I worried I would not make it through school, but I am proud I did."

"Were you treated terribly because of your race?"

"Every cadet at the Point thinks he is being treated terribly at one time or the other. I would never blame my race for tough times. We all have such times. You obviously have lived through your own. I am writing a book about my experiences at West Point." Why did he tell her that? He had been very close-mouthed about the project.

"You are serious? When will it be finished? Do you have a publisher?"

"I am nearly done. I hope to have some evenings when I am not in the field. I need about thirty evenings. And yes, I have a publisher in New York who will publish it and pay royalties, but I do get an advance."

"That is so impressive."

"Writing takes more persistence than brains. I think some will find the book very boring. Could I ask you not to mention a word to anyone else, at least until the book is published and released?"

"If that is what you wish, my lips are sealed."

They talked for several hours, and unconsciously moved nearer to each other as they spoke. Mollie's eyes closed, and he could see she was struggling to stay awake. "It's alright if you nap a spell."

She nodded and leaned her head against his shoulder, dropping off to sleep almost instantly. He did not mind, welcomed her closeness but worried some about what others might think. The privates riding on each side of the stagecoach could see easily through the window openings, and he was already aware of the speed of gossip at military installations. His worry was deferred when sleep claimed him as well.

Chapter 15
The Grim Reaper Waits

THE STAGE PULLED in at a relay station early afternoon. The horse teams were exchanged for fresh horses here, and passengers and escorts could use the privies and draw fresh water from the well. They were served dried beef sandwiches and beans at a crude table inside the station, and a pot of hot coffee and tin cups were placed on the table for use by the diners.

Red spoke as they ate. "Dusk will be coming on when we get to the overnight station. They'll feed you there. Soldiers will need their pup tents next to the coach. Me and Roddy will stretch out on top. Y'all been told that. Two rooms for passengers to sleep in. Men in one, ladies in the other. Guess you two got private rooms tonight. Soldiers got to work out shifts for guard duty."

The two soldiers said nothing, but Flipper could see the fatigue on their faces. Neither could be more than eighteen years old. Riley, a chunky, ruddy-faced kid, looked especially tired. Edwards, a trim, darker lad, appeared to be holding up well enough.

Flipper said, "We'll talk after we get there. I can take a shift or two. I can sleep in the coach while we're traveling."

He turned to Red. "I'm not sure of my authority here, but I think the gold box should be moved inside the station tonight. It would be easier to guard the doors and windows than the stagecoach. We can choose a good place after we get there."

"Lieutenant, y'all can be in charge of the dang gold if you like. I just want to drive my teams." Flipper welcomed command. He still could not believe the mere token force assigned to the stagecoach.

"I'll assume responsibility then. First off, I would like the outriders to move in nearer to the coach, one on each side about ten paces off. You've been riding so far out that we wouldn't hear a warning if you saw anything. You make a better sniper target out there alone as well."

Roddy was glaring at him as he spoke, obviously resenting Flipper's interference. Red had been wary of the young man, and Flipper downright distrusted him now. "Red, do we pass through any towns along the stage route?"

"Nary a one. Tomorrow we'll hit a trading post with a half dozen small houses scattered in the vicinity. I suppose you could call that a town if you like."

So Fort Worth was the nearest town of any size. Any robbers would likely congregate near there and return after their mission. They would gravitate toward supplies, perhaps even a railroad connection. Hopefully, there was no cause for concern, but he concluded that their greatest risk of a strike was during the next leg of their journey when any outlaws could retreat to Fort Worth with their bounty. They likely would not plan to leave living witnesses behind.

"I would like to ride atop the stage for a spell," Flipper said.

"Well," Red said, "I suppose y'all and Roddy could change places for a short while."

"No. We want Roddy in the shotgun spot. I'll just nest on some of the bedrolls and baggage you've got anchored on top."

"No springs. It'll be like riding a bucking bronc."

"I'll be fine."

Red shrugged and got up from the table. "We'd best be moving on if we're going to make the overnight station before dark sets in."

"I'll be leaving you for a bit," Flipper said, as he offered his hand to Mollie to assist her onto the stagecoach.

She accepted his help and climbed into her seat. "You're up to something," she said as he reached for his rifle and dug into his duffel bag, pulling out the scabbard and sword. "Oh my. You are expecting trouble."

"Not necessarily. But a man can't be too careful."

"I wish I had a rifle."

"You can shoot?"

"Since I was ten years old. My daddy taught me. We went hunting together. I'm not the best, but I'm far from the worst, if I say so myself."

"Just a minute." Flipper stepped out of the stage with his sword and rifle cradled in his arms. He called to Red who was in the driver's seat waiting to get the new team moving. "Red, do you have an extra rifle and cartridges up there?"

"Yep. Always got two loaded Winchesters and a double barreled under the driver's seat."

"I'd like to loan one of the Winchesters to Miss Dwyer."

"Sure enough. She ain't the first shooting female I've had aboard my stage." He handed the rifle and an extra cartridge bag down to Flipper, who passed them on to Mollie.

"Can you take orders?" Flipper asked.

Mollie said, "If they make sense."

"You wouldn't make a good soldier."

"Just say 'please.'"

He anchored the scabbard to his belt and with rifle in hand climbed onto the stage top, having to push his way past Roddy perched next to Red on the driver's seat. He suspected the young man was being deliberately uncooperative but said nothing.

An hour later, Flipper could not argue with Red's warning about the comfort of his seating. He had never ridden a bucking bronc, but his body did not have a spot that was not sore. He shifted to find a new position and that was when he saw the dust cloud moving their way. He slipped his Army Colt from its holster, readying it to fire just as Roddy turned in his seat with his rifle aimed at him. Flipper squeezed the trigger and a slug tore into the would-be killer's throat almost simultaneously with the sound of the explosion. Roddy pitched backwards disappearing under the horses' hooves.

Wide-eyed, Red tossed a look over his shoulder.

"Rein in the teams," Flipper hollered. "Rein in. We can't outrun them." A cluster of riders were closing the gap now, and Flipper figured they might have five minutes.

He yelled at the two privates as the stagecoach rolled to a stop. "Under the stage. Fire at will. Riley, when you dismount give me the reins of your bay. We'll catch the other horse later. Mollie, can you hear me?"

She stuck her head through the window. "Yes, I hear you."

"Grab your rifle and get under the stage with the men—please."

Mollie was out of the door in seconds, crawling through the dirt to get positioned under the stage. Flipper leaped off the stage, took the bay gelding's reins from Private Riley and mounted the horse. Six riders, still grouped, were within fifty yards now. Fools, they should have spread out. He reined the horse away from the stagecoach and rode the bay at a fast gallop away from the stagecoach.

The gunfire commenced, and he slowed the gelding and made a sharp turn circling off to the side of the attackers, taking care to stay out of the line of friendly fire. He could see that at least two of the outlaws were down now, but they had veered away, spreading out, making more difficult targets. He pulled out his sword and charged as if leading a company of cavalry.

Flipper was on the first man only moments after he was sighted. The outlaw got off a shot before the sword's blade sliced into his neck, dropping him instantly from his mount. Two other men turned away from the stage and headed for him, guns blazing, one rider with a rifle and the other a pistol. Flipper pushed the bay between the riders with his sword swinging like a scythe. The bloodied bodies of both tumbled from their saddles.

He moved on, seeking out the remaining attacker. He saw him starting to race away just as a shot from underneath the stage took him down. The chaos was over. He dismounted and led his mount over to the stage where the two soldiers, Mollie, and Red were scrambling to their feet.

Mollie's face and dress were covered with dirt, but she still looked stunning as she stood there with Winchester clutched in her hand. Red limped over to him. "Little lady took down that last feller. Didn't know what the hell y'all was up to when you took off like that. Didn't think y'all was the deserting type."

"I figured I'd try a little surprise."

"Y'all surprised them all right. Never seen nothing like it in all my years. Now what do we do with these men and the horses?"

"We don't have time for burying. They all appear to be dead, but we'll need to be sure. We'll drag them to that little gulch off to the right and push what we can in the way of rocks and dirt on them, but I don't think there will be much cover." He turned to the soldiers. "Collect their weapons and anything that might have value. Maybe Red can show us where to stow everything for now. We'll turn it in to the quartermaster when we get to Fort Sill. We'll need to round up the horses, too. Most don't seem to have strayed far. I saw a couple with coiled rope hanging from the saddles. We can make rope lines to lead the critters."

He walked over to speak with Mollie who was standing next to a stagecoach door staring at him. "Are you alright, Mollie?"

"You are crazy. Charging those men with nothing but your sword. They could have shot you down before you got to them."

"But they didn't. Odds were against it. If a man is riding a horse and trying to shoot another man on a horse, it's pure luck if he hits the target. You can't really get a steady aim or sight in on the other man. That only happens in dime novels."

"I just don't know what to make of you."

"Well, that makes two of us. I haven't figured me out yet either. It won't happen today. There's work to be done."

"I'll see if I can help Red. One more question, though. How did you know Roddy was with the outlaws?"

"I didn't for certain till he tried to kill me, but it was just instinct, I guess. I don't think Red trusted him, either. I generally don't like things not based on reason and fact, but I'm learning not to ignore my senses sometimes."

"I take back what I said about you being crazy, but you are strange. I hope we get to know each other better."

"I predict that we shall."

Chapter 16
Jordy

I WAS CROSSING THE parade ground when I saw the stagecoach kicking up dust from the southeastern trail into the fort which was not enclosed within a stockade or walls of any kind. I wondered if Henry might be on the stage, so I ambled over to the limestone quartermaster's building, where passengers disembarked.

I was surprised to find Captain Nicholas Nolan and his new wife, Annie, huddled on the roofed portico and figured they must be awaiting a visitor's arrival. It was a cold January day but still not terrible for this early in the year. We had been spoiled by unseasonably warm weather this winter, but I suspected that further north in my native Kansas the residents were not being treated so kindly.

The stage was due today but had not been expected this early in the afternoon, so I assumed that the soldier who had ridden into the post earlier was one of the escorts sent ahead to alert the quartermaster who would pass the information on to any who needed to know.

When the stage rolled in, I recognized the driver, old Red—I'd never heard a last name—and the lean colored man riding shotgun. Now what in blazes was old Flip doing in that seat? When the teams were reined to a stop, Henry dropped down from his perch, graceful as a nighthawk and opened the stage door. In a few minutes he assisted a pretty, young lady off the stage and then retrieved her bags from the baggage boot at the stage's rear.

By then, Annie Nolan had raced off the porch, calling, "Mollie, Mollie," with tears streaming down her cheeks. The women embraced, and the resemblance told me they were sisters. Captain Nolan stepped off the porch and joined the pair, giving his sister-in-law a proper embrace when the women separated.

Henry was standing a discreet distance back while the family members finished their greetings, and then Mollie summoned him forward. She said, "You must meet Lieutenant Flipper."

Henry immediately set the bags down, stood erect and saluted the captain, who returned the salute and said, "At ease, Lieutenant. We've been looking forward to your arrival. Colonel Grierson has other business this afternoon, but you should report to his office first thing in the morning. Vacant officers' quarters are marked on the door, and you may make your selection."

"And you will dine with us this evening," Annie said. "Seven o'clock. Number three, married officers' quarters."

"I have so many stories to tell you about this man," Mollie said with an impish look on her face.

The ladies liked Henry, and I wondered what stories she had that were fit to share with Annie and her husband. I finally stepped forward. "Henry, I've been watching for you."

He turned toward me. "Jordy, I didn't see you hiding in that big coat."

He always teased me about my dislike of the cold, meaning anything under sixty degrees.

We shook hands, and I grasped his shoulder briefly, knowing that he was not a hugger, not when it came to other males anyhow. "I can show you officers' row, and you can choose a place to set up camp."

"I don't suppose I should leave the stage till the gold shipment is turned over to the proper authority."

Captain Nolan spoke from behind him. "That's the quartermaster's job for now. I will assume responsibility, Lieutenant. The quartermaster has some men who can move the box inside, and I'll see that guards are posted. You are relieved of responsibility, Lieutenant."

"Thank you, sir."

Henry got his duffel and rifle from the stage, and we walked off to find him a place to bunk. At my suggestion and after a promised bribe of coffee and cookies, he claimed a vacancy adjacent to my lodging. After he had put his few things away, Henry came over to my quarters where I had coffee brewing and a few stale cookies I had purchased at the civilian general store that edged the fort grounds.

I had a separate bedroom, but as far as the remaining area was concerned, it was hard to tell where the kitchen ended and the parlor began. I did have the luxury of two leather stuffed chairs just off the doorway with a lamp table in between, and we each claimed one and placed the coffees on the table that already had a hopelessly scarred finish.

I wasn't certain Henry would get around to speaking, so I started the conversation. "It's been a spell. How are your folks back home?"

"They're doing very well. Father's leather business is booming. My mother handles the money and is making good investments. I don't have to worry about them keeping food on their table. Brother Joseph is in college. I think he's looking to do something in the church. He's smart as a whip and knows where he's going. Festus Junior is only ten years old but working in the shop every chance he gets. The folks are seeing he gets an education, but I'm betting he ends up in the business. Emory's only five and Carl, three, so it's anybody's guess for them."

"But I really want to know about Henry."

He shrugged. "Well, I was engaged to a fine woman for a spell, but she decided she wanted no part of the west, and that's where my life will be."

"You didn't waste any time."

"I thought she was the right one and didn't want her to get away. She did. Nothing else to say."

"And you're not going to tell me more."

"Nope. What about your family?"

"They're fine. Little brother Sam will be taking over the ranch someday. Pa made it clear that the operation won't be waiting for me. Big sister Nancy married a nearby rancher. I won't be going home when my time is served here, which will take forever."

"You really don't think the Army will be your career, do you?"

"Not if I can figure out something else to do."

"You are living your father's dream. I don't think that's any kind of life—living somebody else's dreams. We're not obligated to do that. I'm careful about giving other folks advice, but I think you should search out your own dream and then head for it when your Army time is up."

"Yeah, I'll be looking for it, I guess. I need to fill you in on what's happening here. Of course, since you've got dinner with Captain Nolan tonight, you'll probably know more than I do by the time you get back to your bunk. How do you wangle these things?"

"I didn't wangle. I wasn't looking for an invitation, but a man doesn't turn such things down from a superior officer."

"I realize that. Nolan's a good guy. He's assigned to the Tenth regiment like you are. I'll be with the Ninth, but they're never far apart, often headquartered at the same fort like right now. Our paths will be crossing. We're just here while the regiments are being organized and then it's off to someplace else, likely southwest Texas to fight Apache that are still causing trouble."

"I gather Colonel Benjamin Grierson will be commanding the regiments. What do you think of him?"

"I've got nothing but respect for the man. Some still call him 'General.' He was a general of Union volunteers during the Civil War. He was a music teacher before that of all things. After the war, he decided to go regular Army but had to move down a notch in rank. Too dang many generals already, I guess. Anyhow, I'm guessing you'll like Grierson, and he will like you. You'll find some Army smartasses you don't like along the way, but I think that's a ways ahead. Now, why don't you share some of the stories about your travel here that Mollie, whatever her name is, mentioned."

"Not much to share. We ran into some outlaws along the way and had to chase them off. One of them was riding shotgun for us. That's why I ended up on the driver's seat."

"I didn't see any prisoners."

"Didn't take any."

"I give up. The rumors will carry a better story anyhow. Those two soldiers with the stage likely already have it moving through the ranks."

Henry and I talked most of the remaining afternoon, mostly about military things that he had questions about. It was more like an interrogation from my standpoint, but I wouldn't expect anything else from Henry. I was just glad to see him again.

Finally, he had to take his leave, saying he needed to clean up and dust off his dress uniform to be presentable for supper. I told him where the officers' wash house was so he could have a few minutes in a tub with hot water and soap, and a fresh shave if he wanted. An enlisted man was always on duty to tend to whatever he needed. When he departed, I said, "I'll be thinking of you when I'm eating at officers' mess tonight."

Henry just returned a look of annoyance.

Chapter 17
The Nolan-Dwyer Friendship

THE DINNER AT the Nolan residence marked the beginning of a firm friendship between Captain Nicholas Nolan and Lieutenant Henry Flipper and tightened the bond already forming between Mollie Dwyer and the young officer. A roasted beef so tender it fell apart on the fork served with boiled potatoes, gravy, and carrots was a meal Henry would remember without the delicious cherry pie that followed. There was hot coffee on the side, of course, and plenty of relaxed conversation. He felt strangely at ease with these folks.

Small talk dominated till halfway through the meal when the captain abruptly shifted the conversation to the attempted stagecoach robbery. "Mollie told me about the attack on the stage. We can't thank you enough for what you did there. Besides the allotment money for the Comanche, it is very likely those men would have taken Mollie with them, or worse. Regardless, she would not have been here to share the story."

Henry was embarrassed and did not know what to say. "I'm glad I could be helpful."

Nolan chuckled. "I don't think 'helpful' is an adequate description. In any case, I'm certain General Davidson will ask for a written report. Stories are already circulating about the post, likely growing with each telling. You have made a grand entrance."

"General Davidson? I thought Colonel Grierson was in command here."

"Only for the Ninth and Tenth regiments. He will be moving on to Fort Davis. Many address Grierson as 'General,' which was his Civil War rank as head of a regiment of volunteers. After the war, he stayed on with the regular Army but had to accept a rank reduction. He is very respected among the officers and enlisted men here and requested the assignment to organize the Buffalo Soldiers."

"And General Davidson is the commandant of Fort Sill then?"

"General J.W. Davidson, also known as Black Jack Davidson. You will find him quite formal and a bit gruff in comparison to Grierson, but I think he is a fair man and good commandant."

"And you will be with the Ninth and Tenth Regiments?"

"I have been assigned to lead a troop with the Tenth and have requested that you be assigned to my troop. I hope that will be satisfactory with you."

"Of course. I am just glad to be sorting out a few of these things."

"We will probably be among the last to transfer to Fort Davis and will be given work at Fort Sill for some months yet."

Mollie interrupted. "And during that time, I will be very offended if you do not take me horseback riding from time to time."

Henry was not certain how to reply. A colored officer keeping company with a white lady without a chaperone. He was not sure how that might be taken among some on the post.

Annie Nolan saved him. "That's an excellent idea. I suggest you join us every Sunday at noon for dinner. The two of you can go out riding after that, weather permitting, of course."

Nolan said, "That's an excellent idea. You will be expected for Sunday dinner, Mister Flipper."

"Yes, sir."

After they ate, a young woman appeared with a tray to pick up plates and other dinnerware. Annie and Mollie stood to assist, but it was obvious that they were spared certain household chores. "Follow me," the captain said, "I have a few matters I would like to discuss."

As they started to walk away, Annie said, "Nick, you have a half hour. Our guest just arrived. I think he would welcome an early bedtime, and Mollie and I would like to share a bit more of his time before he departs for the night."

"Yes, ma'am."

As they walked into a Spartanly furnished room, devoid of wall hangings and consisting only of a desk, two chairs and a packed bookcase, Nolan said, "We have been married no more than a month now, but you can see who commands the household here. Annie's the prize, though, and my young children adore her. I have a boy and a girl, John and Susie. You will meet them Sunday. We had friends next door look after them this evening." He hesitated, "Would you like a drink? I've got whiskey and a bottle of red wine in the bottom drawer of my desk. Or maybe you aren't a drinking man."

"I seldom touch the spirits, but a glass of wine might be nice tonight." He hated wine only a bit less than whiskey but did not want to come off too strait-laced to his superior officer.

"Grab one of the chairs and sit down while I pour the drinks." He took two bottles from the desk with two whiskey glasses, first pouring the wine before tending to his own whiskey. He handed the glass of wine to Henry. "Sorry, no fancy wineglass." He sat down on the other straight back chair on the same side of the desk as Henry.

"Thank you," Henry said, taking a sip of the wine which was bitter to his taste, but he thought he had avoided wincing.

Nolan said, "May I call you 'Henry' when there are just the two of us? I would like you to call me 'Nick.'"

"Certainly, Captain . . . uh . . . Nick."

"It will take some practice. How is everyone treating you, Henry?"

"Fine. Everyone has been very helpful, and my old friend from West Point, Jordy Dixon, is here and has been showing me around."

"I will speak bluntly, Henry. I know folks don't always treat colored people with respect, and I want you to know you can come to me anytime if anyone gives you a problem."

"Well, thank you, Nick, but I don't anticipate anything that would trigger that. Whenever I encounter unpleasantness of that sort, I'm quite adept at ignoring it. Some folks just don't hit it off so well, and it's not necessarily race."

"I guess I'm a bit more sensitive to these things. I'm Irish, and there are many who have no use for the Irish. I don't have so much of a problem anymore as an Army officer, but as a young man I turned to fisticuffs more than once over what I took to be an Irish slur. I know that what we put up with is a fraction of what colored people endure."

Henry was beginning to understand why Nolan had made the special effort to make him feel welcome. "I will be fine, Nick, but I am very appreciative of the fact that you and your family have made me feel I belong here. You can count on me as a friend and junior officer."

They talked Army business for the remainder of their conversation with Nolan filling him in on secrets that would make life easier, especially regarding people and those who might be most helpful and others who were generally uncooperative. It was over when Annie appeared in the doorway with arms folded across her bosom. "It has been nearly an hour, Nick."

The husband smiled. "I've been waiting for this young man to empty his wine glass. We'll be right there."

Henry took a quick swallow and placed the empty glass on the desk. "Finished."

They joined the ladies in the parlor for another half hour before Henry announced that he should probably get back to his quarters and complete unpacking. He thanked the hosts for their hospitality, and Mollie stepped out onto the porch with him as he left.

"I'm glad you could join us, Henry. I hope we can be good friends. After our adventure on the stagecoach ride, I feel like I have known you forever."

"Well, I will be seeing you Sundays for sure, and I'm committed to horseback rides. I do welcome the opportunity to get to know you better, Mollie."

Mollie started to move to him as if to embrace and then hesitated and stepped back. "Goodnight, Henry."

"Goodnight, Mollie."

As Henry walked back to his quarters, he could not erase Mollie from his thoughts. So pretty and vivacious, obviously intelligent, too. Might he find a future with this woman? He had best step away from any such notions. Color barriers could be broken. He had proved that. But some took longer than others to tear down.

Chapter 18
Settling In

HENRY HAD EXPECTED to spend a few weeks at Fort Sill before moving on, but his stay turned into many months and eventually extended to more than a year. At his first weekly dinner with the Nolans, Annie Nolan invited him to board at their residence.

"We have a cook," she said, "and weekly maid service for the laundry and house cleaning. I have never been so spoiled. It would obviously be no additional burden for Mollie and me, and we love your company. I promise that we Irish won't be that difficult to live with."

Annie appeared to put her invitation as more plea than offer, and he did not see how he could turn her down. He accepted, against his better judgment, and agreed to move into the bedroom that was two doors away from Mollie's room with the captain's study separating the rooms. He worried about what other officers and soldiers might think in terms of his boarding with the captain of his troop.

That afternoon, he and Mollie took their first ride together. Henry rode a big sorrel gelding, and Mollie, dressed in ladies' riding britches, was astride a smaller, albeit more spirited, dappled gray gelding. She had insisted on a challenging critter, which did not surprise him. They rode no more than two miles distant from the post taking care not to cross into Comanche reservation lands, then moved along the common ground retained by the government for future fort expansion.

After an initial surge at near racing speed, Mollie, who was setting the pace, reined in her mount to a slow gallop and eventually a walk. Riding side by side, they could now converse. Mollie said, "I guess we will be seeing a lot of each other."

"It appears so, but I won't be in your way much. I am getting a good list of assignments, some that will take me away for days at a time. I will see if I can get my clothes and gear moved over to the Nolan house tomorrow evening."

"Can I help?"

"Uh, there is not that much. And it might cause unnecessary talk if you were going in and out of my quarters. I'm sure my friend Jordy will help." And Jordy would likely have plenty to say about the move.

Mollie said, "And our living in the same house and taking horseback rides together will not cause talk?"

"Your point is well taken. I will see how it goes with my living in the captain's residence. General Davidson has scheduled me for the day after tomorrow to discuss an engineering project, which will likely keep me busy for a spell. As for the horseback rides, that will be your decision."

"The decision has been made. As often as we can."

That evening Henry informed Jordy of his new living arrangements. He was not surprised at his friend's reaction.

"Flip, nine times out of ten you're smarter than me. I'll listen to you before any man. But this is the one time, you've got a broken cog in your brain. I worry that a part of your brain has slipped below your belt. You can't live in the same house as this Mollie. You get caught in her bed—or yours if she crawls into it—and your career is done."

"It's not like that. Mollie's a friend, that's all."

"Right now, maybe. But I've seen that pretty gal. And sleeping a few doors away from her. No man's got that kind of resistance."

"One does. If my feelings ever become inappropriate, I will move out. I would never bring scandal to Captain Nolan or his family."

Jordy stared at him. "Yeah, you might be that one man. I guarantee you that I'm not. So you want to move tomorrow night?"

"Yep."

"Alright. I'll help. That ought to be an easy enough job. By the way, I got some news today. Another week, and I'll be pulling out."

"You're not deserting, I hope."

"Not yet anyhow. The Ninth is moving down to Fort Concho. We'll be there a spell to finish getting organized, whatever that means. I was told that's what we were doing here. After that, my first lieutenant thinks we might be moving on to Fort Elliot. Your Tenth Cavalry will join us sometime, but God knows when or where. The Army sure as hell doesn't have it figured out yet."

"Well, I'll miss you, Jordy, but I suspect we'll meet up again in a month or two."

"Or five or six. I'll write, though, and let you know where to send those twenty-page books you write."

"I can't help it. When I start writing, I can't stop."

"I'm not complaining, I enjoy your letters, but I can't translate once in a while if I don't have a dictionary near-by."

"Well, I daresay yours are a lot more entertaining. They're always good for a few laughs, and I get quite engrossed in some of your tales. You keep me guessing on how much is truth and how much is part of those dime novels you store in your head."

"I don't know for sure myself sometimes. I've told you I live in two worlds. The real one, and the one that's in my head. I'm hoping that someday I can get paid for the one in my head."

Henry rarely spoke of it, but he knew Jordy was aware that he was writing his own book based upon West Point experiences that he hoped to complete by midsummer. He already had a publisher, but now he needed to provide the words. He had a compulsion to reduce thoughts and experiences to writing in diaries. He also had shared some of these with Anna White, his former fiancée, under no illusions that they would reconcile.

The next evening, with Jordy's assistance, Henry was settled in the Nolan home. Annie, of course, invited Jordy for supper, and they were joined by the young children, John and Susan, with Captain Nolan sitting at the head of the long dining table. It was a relaxed meal with friendly banter, and Henry felt like he was with family again. The evening did trigger a bit of nostalgia for his parents and home in Georgia. He was aware that it would likely be years before he saw his family, but he had not returned to Georgia during his four years at West Point. This was the life he had chosen.

Henry and Jordy talked for a spell on the porch before Jordy headed for his quarters. Just before he stepped off the porch, Jordy said, "Forgive me my friend, if I'm a bit jealous. These folks have adopted you as kin. I might have been wrong for the first time in my life. This might work out just fine for you."

Chapter 19
Flipper's Ditch

ENRY HAD A comfortable relationship with Colonel Grierson, who commanded the Ninth and Tenth regiments of Buffalo Soldiers, but he had never met General "Black Jack" Davidson until today. An orderly had escorted him into the general's office where the commandant was seated at his desk, his eyes focused on a book, probably some military manual, Henry assumed.

The general was a slender man with dark hair and a thick mustache with tips that met up with a short beard that ran along his jawline. His face was weatherworn like that of a field officer, but Henry judged him not to be more than fifty years old. Henry stood at attention, uncertain what to do. He did not want to interrupt the commandant's strategizing.

Finally, Davidson looked up. "Who are you?"

"Second Lieutenant Henry Flipper reporting for duty, sir." He saluted, and the general, remaining in his chair, returned what he took to be a sloppy salute.

"At ease, Lieutenant, and be seated." He nodded toward one of the two straight-back chairs in front of his desk.

Henry sat down and waited for the general to speak. Davidson held up the book he had been reading. "Ever read Jake West, Lieutenant?"

"Uh, no sir."

"He's better than Ned Buntline. You've read him, of course. He's the best-selling dime novelist in the country. West ought to be."

"I'm afraid I haven't read Buntline either, sir."

"Damn it, son. Your education has been seriously neglected. I'm going to send one of Buntline's books and one of West's with you. I will expect your honest opinion about who you think is best."

"Yes, sir."

"Now, what were you here for?"

"I was told you might have an engineering project for me, sir."

"Oh, yes. You've seen those damned ponds and pools of water all over the end of the camp? Smelly, dirty things."

"Yes, sir, I have."

"The Sill doctors think they're a health problem besides being danged unsightly. We have a lot of malaria here. Some of the docs think that these pools could be the blame."

"I've heard of such theories, sir."

"You are an engineer, and my file says that you were one of the best in your class—that and the languages. You might be useful here."

"I hope so, sir."

"Well, Mister Flipper, I want you to figure out how to dry out those pools."

"They would need to be drained to someplace, sir, to a decent sized river."

"I'm guessing you would have to go to the Red River."

"That's the border between Texas and Indian Territory. I was studying that on my maps. I'm estimating a forty-mile journey."

"You figure it out. Captain Nolan will have a full troop at your disposal. I would like to see it done soon. The quartermaster will be directed to provide whatever you need. I want you to start tomorrow. You will be free of other assignments until the project is finished. You are dismissed now, Lieutenant."

Flipper stood and saluted. "Thank you, sir."

Davidson waved him away.

That evening following supper, Henry spoke with Captain Nolan about his new assignment as the two sat in the parlor in front of the crackling fireplace. Nolan said, "I knew the assignment was coming down, but General Davidson wanted to meet you personally and convey the order. You carry some fame on your shoulders, and he could not have you posted here and be unable to say that he had never spoken with you. I fear that the project he has in mind may be impossible to accomplish, but I never had that much enthusiasm for the engineering side of the academy. My grades in those subjects were barely passing."

Henry said, "I've thought about that situation before. The big problem is the distance. Essentially, we need a big drainage ditch that connects the pools and flows to the Red River. Elevation will be most important. Obviously, water will not drain upslope. I hope the quartermaster can find surveying equipment in his inventory and plenty of shovels. The soldiers of our Tenth Cavalry troop will not be pleased with the task I have in mind. They cannot do this work from horseback."

"They've had it a bit too easy here, and as far as I'm concerned it beats dodging Apache arrows. With the Civil War and the Red River War against the Comanche, I'm not so hungry for combat anymore. I'll gladly take a shovel myself. General Davidson wants the project completed before rainy season hits late spring. He said we can alternate some of the other troops with ours, and we can have additional troops working at the same time if necessary to complete the project. I am just to tell him what we need."

"First, I must ride the distance to the Red River and map out the location of the shallow ponds. I must do some survey work and make elevation calculations. It would make no sense to connect every pond between here and the Red River. I am thinking we should drain every pond within the fort boundaries and five miles beyond. Do you think that would satisfy the general?"

"I'm certain it would. I will make him aware of what you propose, but I don't think he will care if the ponds within sight are drained, and the surgeons quit complaining."

"I will ride to the Red River tomorrow after I leave a list of survey equipment needs with the quartermaster. I would like to take two soldiers along who will be assisting me with surveys and supervision of the project. Any suggestions?"

Nolan thought for a moment. "Sergeant Milo Murphy for one. The soldiers generally respect him—or fear him—and will obey his orders even though he always gives them with a smile. He can think for himself, and you don't have to explain a task to him more than once. Then I would recommend Corporal Jimmy Mitchell. He's a smart young man and can read and write. I think he picked up an eighth-grade education somewhere along the way. He's only twenty-two, and I think will be a first sergeant within a few years, a master sergeant someday if he stays in the Army."

"Murphy and Mitchell then. I would like to have them ride with me tomorrow."

"I'll see that they get their orders. You will be visiting the quartermaster, and you will be out three or four days if you are going to the Red River and studying the terrain along the way. I'll direct Murphy and Mitchell to round up food and other supplies for the trip. I suggest you have noon dinner here and leave right after."

"That makes sense. With luck, I may be able take some surveying equipment with me, but most of that work will come later."

Chapter 20
The Ditch Diggers

THE THREE CAVALRYMEN rode away from Fort Sill on the mission nobody had signed up for. Sergeant Milo Murphy, a stocky, brown-faced man with a perpetual smile, led a pack mule loaded with food and camp gear. Another mule carrying mostly survey equipment followed Corporal Jimmy Mitchell, a wiry, raw-boned young man with a dark face that suggested his African blood was undiluted.

At first, they rode at little more than a walk while Henry explained his plan. He said, "I want to start at the river and work my way back. Mostly, I just want to see what we are dealing with. Keep in mind that we have one objective and that is to drain the ponds in the vicinity of

Fort Sill and see that the water gets to the Red River or disappears and dries up before it gets there."

Murphy said, "Sir, are we going to be digging a ditch all the way from the fort to the river?"

"That's what I want to find out about during this trip. I'm hoping we will come across some creeks or gulleys that feed the river that will do that work for us. We may split up as we move south so that we can follow some of these possibilities. Have either of you crossed the Red River?"

Murphy said, "We both did, sir, when we rode up from Concho to join the fellers gathering up at Sill. I wasn't giving no thought at the time to sending water from Sill down that way. There was some big gulleys and such, but danged if I gave a thought to where they run to."

Mitchell said, "I know what you're looking for, sir. I ain't sure, but there was one that might be what you're looking for. We didn't come this way, but it looked to be cutting southwest away from the fort. We were a long way out at the time, so I couldn't guess in miles."

"Well, I guess we'll just have to keep our eyes open."

A few hours later, they came upon a gulley that was perhaps ten feet deep at this juncture and appeared to be shallowing as it wound northeasterly, indicating it would not be taking in a lot of water before it reached this area.

Flipper guessed that they were less than ten miles from the outer boundaries of Fort Sill.

They reined in their mounts while he perused the terrain around the gulley. "Corporal," he asked Mitchell, "could this be the gulley you saw?"

"Sir, I just can't be certain, but I think it could be."

"We'll stay together for now and follow this and see where it takes us."

Late afternoon, the riders still had their gulley, and it appeared to be headed south toward the Red River.

"Lieutenant, we followed the gulley from the river to this point and then veered away and went straight north. This is the one." He turned to Murphy, "Don't you think this is it, Sarge?"

"Yep. You're right, Jimmy, as usual."

Henry said, "Let's set up camp here for the night. I want to see if I can get some survey readings before dark. I'll finish at sunrise before we move on if need be. I'll need one man to enter some numbers in my book and help with the sightings. The other can start setting up camp and figure out something to eat. Volunteers?"

Murphy said, "I'm the cook. I know my numbers if they ain't too big. And I read and write at a snail's pace. Jimmy's your survey man."

The next day they continued following the ravine which deepened some as they moved south. Other smaller gulleys fed into it and eventually an occasional stream or small creek until it became a permanent watercourse. When they reached the Red River that night and set up camp again, Henry was confident he had found the outlet for excess waters from Fort Sill.

The next day they rode easterly along the north bank of the Red River, confirming there was no outlet more promising than the initial discovery. When they turned back north, Henry asked his companions about the limestone he saw scattered about the land. "I'm looking for a source of limestone at one or two places where we could mine the rock to line the drainage ditches I want to construct. Have either of you seen anything like that near the post?"

Corporal Mitchell said, "No more than two miles northeast, sir, there's mostly hill country for as far as you can see. I saw several caved away bluffs with limestone piles at the bottom waiting for harvest. I suppose that's where the stone for some of the buildings came from. I can show you when we get back to the post."

"Yes, I'd like you to do that, Corporal."

They camped within a half day's ride of the fort, so Flipper could map and survey the southernmost pooling areas on the way back. The plan was formulating in his mind as he took his readings that were catalogued by Mitchell. Murphy helped with the prism pole when Henry was working at the tripod and transit with the theodolite instrument measuring angles and elevations.

When they rode into the fort at near dusk, Henry advised the men to meet him at the stable at nine o'clock the next morning to visit the limestone hills and complete the survey of the pooling areas within or near the post boundaries. "You have both been very helpful. I will need you to see this project through."

The Nolans had already eaten supper when Henry returned to his lodging place, but Annie insisted he sit down at the dining table while she warmed the leftovers, and both Mollie and Captain Nolan joined him while he ate.

Nolan asked, "Will you be able to solve General Davidson's concerns with the ponds?"

"I don't see why not. I have some more survey work tomorrow and then I will need two days to draw my plans and diagrams to present to the general. How much time do we have to beat the worst of the rains?"

"We're nearing the end of February. Rains will start in April."

"The entire project cannot be finished in that time, but we'll get the pooling on the post grounds first and build an unlined ditch immediately to get that water away."

"Unlined?"

"We will line those ditches on and nearer the post with limestone, so they will last for years. Otherwise, they will cave in and wash."

"That will take a lot of men."

"Yes. The general indicated we could requisition the men we need. We'll work six days a week, grant the men Sundays off. I hope they might be given some furlough time when the project is completed."

"I hope this works."

"It will work."

Mollie finally spoke. "Sundays off. Does that mean the supervisor of the project can join a lady for a horseback ride from time to time?"

"No promises. But I will certainly try."

Mollie turned to Nolan. "Nick, I think the captain should order the lieutenant to take Sundays off for a bit of leisure."

Nolan rolled his eyes. "I don't think the captain will be issuing orders to the lieutenant anytime soon. Henry, use my office here in the house while you are doing your drawings and calculations. Tell me what you need in the way of manpower, and I will see to that."

"I plan to use Seargent Murphy to direct the workers, and Corporal Mitchell will supervise to see that specifications are being met. We will need thirty to forty men from dawn to dusk, giving them a break for noon dinner, of course. Some will be mining limestone, and we will need wagons and teams for hauling the rock to the ditches. If there are soldiers with stonemason skills, they would be especially helpful."

Mollie said, "I don't find this very exciting. Excuse me, I am going to read for a while before bedtime."

The first phase of ditch construction took till shortly past the first of April, and the morning of completion, Flipper was surprised at the site by a visit from General Black Jack Davidson and two officials from the War Department. He was explaining an adjustment that needed to be made to the outlet from one of the dry pools to Corporal Mitchell when the general and his guests appeared.

When he saw the general, he came to attention and saluted, "Good morning, sir. This is a nice surprise," he lied.

"Lieutenant. I took a chance and gave you all the rope you wanted on your ditches, so I haven't been breathing down your neck. I've got Mister Downs, an assistant secretary from the War Department, and Mister Carpenter, a project inspector here for this week, and I thought they should see this project."

"Pleased to meet you, gentlemen," Henry said.

Both sober-faced men nodded but ignored his extended hand. He assumed that the paunchy, balding man with the brushy, gray mustache was the assistant secretary and that the short, young stick-like man was the project inspector, Carpenter.

"Would you kindly explain how you expect to drain these pools when the rain comes?" Carpenter said. "Water doesn't flow uphill."

"The pools will drain, sir. The slope is more than adequate. The lay of the land is such here that the incline is an illusion."

"Bullshit. You've got the ditches trying to climb hills."

"Everything has been surveyed and laid out carefully."

The assistant secretary said, "You've got it all looking very nice with the rock lined trenches and all, but I fear Mister Carpenter is right. The water is not going anyplace."

General Davidson said, "Lieutenant, I truly hope you are right. The Army has invested a lot of money and man hours in what everybody is calling 'Flipper's Ditch.' And you propose to spend another two months extending and refining the project. If this doesn't work with the first big rain, we are going to reevaluate the whole danged thing."

"And we will insist on a reprimand of some sort on your record," Carpenter said.

Henry did not know what else he could say. He did not wish to raise the general's ire with a fuss. He just said, "I understand."

The visitors strolled along the edge of the ditch for a spell before they veered away to pester some other unsuspecting soul. He stood there for some minutes surveying the maze of ditches, some spanned by little stone bridges creating a park-like atmosphere.

Corporal Jimmy Mitchell startled him from behind when he spoke. "Sir, I heard what they said."

Flipper turned around and faced the young soldier. "Corporal, I didn't know you were here."

"I was coming with a few questions, sir, but when I saw the general and his bigwigs, I stayed put over by those big oaks. The ditch will work, sir. I've got no doubt. It will work."

"Maybe I should talk to Quanah Parker and see if his Comanche will do a big rain dance for us. I'd sure like to test the system while those bureaucrats are here, however it comes out."

Chapter 21
The Test

THAT NIGHT HENRY was awakened by a clap of thunder and flash of lightning. He sat up in bed and listened to the splatter of rain against his window as a ferocious west wind shook the house. The ditch's test had arrived. He lay back, listening to the rumbling skies and hammering of the rain outside, thinking he would fall asleep and check the ponds in the morning.

But sleep eluded him, and after several hours, he got up, pulled on a flannel civilian shirt and stepped into cold britches and went to the kitchen to see if the cookstove was still hot enough to brew some coffee. He was surprised when he found Mollie, wrapped in a long robe, in front of the stove already taking on the task.

"What took you so long?" Mollie asked. "I've been expecting you for an hour—and, yes, there is plenty of coffee for you and sweet rolls from the Army bakery. Why don't you go feed the parlor fireplace and then come back here. We can sit at the kitchen table. It's cozier and warmer in here at the coal stove right now."

When he returned, he sat down where she had his frosted, cherry-filled pastry and a steaming mug of coffee waiting. Mollie seemed to be staring at him when he took his first sip from the mug. "What?"

"I've never seen you looking the way you do now. You are always in uniform, every button in place. You are even barefooted."

He was uncertain how to take her remark and shrugged. "I didn't expect to encounter a young lady out here this time of night."

She giggled. "Oh, I didn't mean to sound like you look terrible or anything. I rather like the disheveled look. It's different. You even seem more relaxed. Lord, I must look awful." She brushed her fingers through her thick hair.

He smiled. "Disheveled suits you, too." And he thought he would like to take Miss Disheveled to bed at this very minute.

She rescued him from the direction he felt the conversation was leading. "You were thinking about Flipper's Ditch, weren't you?"

"You have tagged the project with my name, too?"

"Everybody calls it that. You are famous. Perhaps, you have constructed a national monument."

"Or a national disaster, which I suspect is the hope of some, especially a few government bureaucrats visiting the post. But, yes, when the storm woke me, the ditch is all I could think about."

"Nick told Annie and me about the War Department men. They are causing problems for everybody in the post. Nothing is being done right according to those two. He mentioned that neither man has ever served in the Army."

They ate and drank their coffee silently for several minutes before Henry spoke again. "I would really like to go check the ditches."

"Don't be foolish. The wall clock says it is half past three. It is still pouring rain. Won't you be able to judge better if the ponds have more time to fill and you can see in the light of day?"

He sighed. "That will be another three hours, but I guess you're right."

"I will stay up with you, and we will go together to watch the water draining away from the ponds. In the meantime, we will drink a lot of coffee and talk."

He never tired of this woman's company and given that his preferred alternative was not an option, he would take her suggestion. They talked until a bit of light sifted through the curtains, and then they both went to their bedrooms to get dressed.

"I have an extra Army poncho for you," Henry said. "After I'm dressed, I'll go to the stable and get us two mounts and bring them back to the house. There doesn't seem to be any lightning now, just steady rainfall."

It took over an hour for Henry to get dressed and retrieve the horses, and when he returned, he found Mollie waiting under the shelter of the porch roof. She trudged through the mud in her riding boots, took her horse's reins and swung into the saddle.

"You lead the way," she said.

They rode the horses at a walk and reached the nearest pond in twenty minutes. Henry's stomach was turning somersaults as they approached the first cluster of ponds.

"They're draining," Mollie yelled. "Look, the water is rushing through the trenches."

Yes, the water appeared to be moving just like he planned. The nearest pond would clearly empty and dry out in a few days' time. He dismounted and started leading his gelding around the perimeter of the ponds and across the stone bridge that spanned one of the ditches.

Mollie moved up beside him, leading her own mount. "The trenches are like a giant spider web moving water to the center to a bigger channel that carries the water downstream."

"That is the idea. Then the other ponds will connect and then some of the water will just fan out onto the prairie and dry out while the main trench carries the drainage to natural watercourses that will transport it to the Red River."

She released her horse's reins and moved to Henry and embraced him tightly. Startled at first, he responded by releasing his own horse and wrapping his arms about her.

She said, "You should be so proud." She placed her hand behind his neck and gently pulled his head down to her. Their lips met in a lingering kiss that sent Henry to the edge of heaven.

She eased away, seemingly not embarrassed by the moment. "I assume you want to check Flipper's Ditch farther downstream."

He did not want the magic of this moment to disappear, but his good sense finally prevailed. "Yes, I would like to go on a mile or two, if you don't mind."

"Of course not. We're both soaked anyhow, and I'm going to get a good scolding from Annie whenever I show up."

Chapter 22
Jordy

OLD FLIP MADE his mark at Fort Sill, but not so much for the kind of soldiering he had in mind when he headed west. With the success of Flipper's Ditch, General Davidson assigned him to other projects that required engineering skills, the most notable being construction of a road from Fort Sill to the railroad at Gainesville, Texas, more than a hundred miles distant.

The white folks in Gainesville loved Flipper and treated him and the other colored men like royalty while they were there. Flip told me they rarely had to prepare a meal while working out of Gainesville. The ladies were delivering to their camp via less enthusiastic husbands more than enough delicious foods to fill their bellies. Several of the women checked in every other morning with the camp cook to set a menu for the next few days. The cook made coffee and spread out the food on his serving counters and otherwise enjoyed a lot of extra sleep while they camped near the town.

Henry somehow had a way of dealing with the civilian population wherever he was posted, and this was in the deep South, mind you. The merchants with whom he became acquainted were especially fond of him, and most seemed color blind when it came to his race. There were exceptions, of course, but Flip never once complained. He just chose not to do business with those who did not welcome him. Many of such contacts involved military purchases, and those men and women were cutting off their own noses.

Flip enjoyed the assignments that took him to the Comanche reservation. Occasionally, Comanche warriors were allowed to leave the reservation to hunt, but after some of the hunting parties brought back horses and cattle stolen from white ranchers, the Army required that a small contingent of soldiers accompany any warriors on their hunting trip.

Henry and a half dozen or so of Tenth Cavalry soldiers were often given this task because of his Spanish proficiency. Some Comanche spoke rudimentary Spanish because the Mexican side of the Rio Grande was formerly a refuge from white soldiers and offered other raiding opportunities, especially for harvesting extra wives or slaves. The captives brought Spanish to the villages, so that communication with outsiders might include a mix of English, Spanish and Comanche. I am certain Flip had no idea where his language skills would eventually lead him.

Henry ended up spending almost two years at Fort Sill before the Tenth was ordered to move to Fort Elliott in the Texas panhandle west of Fort Sill and a bit north. Our paths crossed briefly in the intervening months, but usually our time was eaten up by the mission we shared. I was stationed with the Ninth at Fort Davis far to the southwest, almost a hundred miles south of the Pecos River and less than that to the Mexican border. He wrote that he expected Elliot to be a brief stop before the Tenth joined the Ninth at Fort Davis, and I looked forward to opportunities to spend more time for real conversation on occasion.

I wondered if he knew that Flipper's Ditch was famous among troops stationed in the Southwest. I was curious also if he was aware of the gossip spreading about the "nigger and the white woman." There was no doubt that most were convinced that Flip was getting regular pokes with Mollie Dwyer. There were no written rules prohibiting such relationships, but a strong majority among the soldiers likely condemned such things between colored men and whites. In our correspondence during this time, he rarely mentioned Mollie, and he wrote only briefly of the drainage system he was constructing at the fort.

What worried me some was that I knew Captain Nolan would be with the Tenth, and I feared his wife and Mollie would join him in married officer's housing. I hated to see Henry's career harmed by these rumors, and I was sure he would continue to nourish them. His fellow officers seemed more tolerant than the rank and file of white soldiers. I assume that all but a few colored troopers would not care, maybe even get a certain satisfaction out of the disgruntlement of the whites.

I do know that Henry came to love Fort Sill and hated to leave it. In his writings, he even admits to shedding a few tears upon departure.

Chapter 23
Fort Elliott

HENRY WAS NOT surprised when informed that his first assignment at Fort Elliott was to survey and map the boundaries and location of the buildings. Captain Nolan was the highest-ranking officer at the post when they arrived in the fall of 1879 and thereby became commanding officer until displaced by someone of higher rank. The fact that he knew Henry hungered for other assignments, however, did not deter Nolan from ordering the task completed. He had found demands for the survey on the commanding officer's desk that had evidently gone unheeded, likely because of the absence of a qualified surveyor on the post.

Nolan appointed Henry Post Adjutant, which made him the senior officer on the post, and this pleased the young lieutenant, figuring the designation would look good on his record when future promotions were considered. Annie and the children, as well as Mollie, did join them at Fort Elliott, but because of the small house occupied by the family, Henry claimed his separate quarters. He was grateful for that development, because he sensed that some officers assumed favoritism because of the living arrangement.

He enjoyed being near Mollie, but he had reached the limits of enduring their platonic situation, especially under the same roof. Maybe he could now get her out of his head. Occasional horseback rides together continued, but his new responsibilities made these less frequent, and he had to deal with a bit of pouting when he was forced to turn down her requests.

He thought more than once that any uneasiness between them could be resolved by marriage, but they had never advanced to romance beyond a special occasion kiss or embrace. Increasingly, he doubted she would marry a colored man, but there was an indefinable bond between them. Someday, he would gently broach the subject in a hypothetical way.

As winter approached, Henry was summoned to Captain Nolan's office. When he entered, he came to attention and saluted because they always maintained formalities for official business.

The captain returned the salute. "Be seated, Mister Flipper."

They sat down at Nolan's warped, wobbly desk. "First, I want to thank you for the surveying and mapping you did. This will interest someone at the War Department, likely someone who has never set foot on an Army post. They will probably wonder why we have no walls sketched in or defensive barriers of some kind."

"There are none."

"No. I understand this fort has always been something of a way station or supply depot for the military. Troops stationed here were called out when Indians raided nearby ranches, but there has never been an attack on the fort, thankfully, and it appears that these days such a possibility is beyond remote. I wanted to make you aware that we have received orders for transfer to Fort Davis, but we are not to be there till just after the first of March when a campaign against Victorio and his Apache bands will begin."

"That's good news, sir."

"I hope so. It could be a very dangerous mission. Men will die."

Henry was thinking of the opportunity for real soldiering. He had not considered the downside. "I assume the Ninth will be there."

"Yes. They have been at Fort Davis with Colonel Grierson for most of the year, as well as a regiment of Buffalo infantry. The Buffalo Soldiers are expected to see most of the action. But that is not what I wanted to speak to you about."

"Sir?"

"I want you to plot a trail for us to take when we transfer to Fort Davis. Select a half dozen men to accompany you. As you move south, especially after crossing the Pecos, Apache attacks are possible, and there are still a few renegade Comanche bands in that country. It is not a journey to make alone. We are talking about a three hundred or so mile march. You will stop at Fort Concho, because I am told that when we make our move near the end of February, a company or two of infantry will join us there."

"I will be gone a spell."

"A month or more would not surprise me. You and your men will want to take winter gear. You can add to that at Concho and resupply on food and the like there. I will send a letter of authority."

"When would you like me to depart, sir?"

"Day after tomorrow. You will want to notify your six men, and I am betting Sergeant Milo Murphy and Corporal Jimmy Mitchell are among them."

Flipper surrendered a rare smile. "You have won your bet, sir."

Chapter 24
Trail To Fort Davis

FLIPPER AND HIS six soldiers rode away from Fort Elliott on an unseasonably warm late November day. Before they departed, Captain Nolan informed Henry that he was expected for Christmas dinner if they returned before then. The invitation reminded him of his West Point days during which he did not once return to Georgia to visit family. Neither was he ever invited to a classmate's home for the holidays or to a professor's residence for Christmas dinner as were some of the students who were unable to unite with family.

He always shrugged such things off to oversight and rejected wallowing in self-pity. Still, he could not deny the occasional stings that he felt at such times. His Army service for the most part had been free of such experiences. The Nolans and many other officers and their families had generally welcomed him. There were exceptions, of course, but those officers were simply cold and unfriendly. For all he knew that might just be their nature, and he never dwelt upon it. He sensed that some white enlisted men, not all, resented taking orders from a colored officer, but fortunately most of his responsibilities lay with the Buffalo Soldiers. Bottom line: he loved the Army.

The scouting party included Sergeant Milo Murphy, Corporal Jimmy Mitchell, and four privates, one a seasoned soldier who had been a first sergeant several times before working his way down the ranks following drunken brawls. Murphy had vouched for Stretch Hooper, noting that the man had been an escaped slave who lived with the Tonkawa for some years before hiring on with several Tonkawa warriors as a scout for General Ranald Slidell Mackenzie during the Red River War against the Comanche.

Hooper was a scarecrow figure of a man several inches taller than Henry, with a tuft of chin whiskers that made Henry think of a billy goat. He was easy going and good natured, except when the bottle got the best of him, Murphy warned. Henry did not intend to offer drinking opportunities to the men on the journey. They had a job to do and then they would head back to Fort Elliott without delay.

Henry rode the Spanish dun stallion he had purchased from an officer being transferred, the only stallion in the regiment and gentle as a lamb. He smiled at the remembrance of Mollie's complaining because he was taking her favorite riding horse with him. He wondered if the stallion would be a suitable wedding gift if the couple should someday make a lifetime match. He still had not broached that subject. It was not his nature to defer action. This discussion was an exception.

The party also led two spare mounts, as well as two pack mules loaded with food and cooking and camping supplies. They moved at a steady, but slow pace, wanting to spare both animals and horses for the long journey ahead. He could judge distance only by saddle time and estimated that they covered thirty miles the first day.

They stayed with well-established trails, changing courses only where rock cave-ins or flooding had destroyed former paths, occasionally backtracking and finding another route. In addition to at least several hundred soldiers, many wagons would be accompanying the troops, and their passageway must be secured. Still, Henry wondered if Captain Nolan had not given him the assignment just to keep him occupied with more traditional cavalry tasks.

They arrived at Fort Concho and the adjacent town of San Angelo nearly ten days after leaving Fort Elliott. Henry had hoped to make the journey in a week's time but reasoned that the route back would already be mapped out and planned, so that would cut travel time upon their return.

The fort had been a center of activity for the Indian wars and Buffalo Soldiers in particular. Most orders for troop movements, although issued by field officers, were first conveyed by the commanding officer at the fort. The Buffalo Soldiers often had lengthy stopovers there.

Henry decided they would take the opportunity to rest horses and mules and replenish food supplies with a two-night stay at Concho before moving on. He also hoped to fish for information about the journey ahead while there. He struck a gold mine of information when the post adjutant turned out to be a friendly, helpful sort. Captain Frederick Gerlach, a fair-complected, blond man of average size who spoke with a slight German accent was not only welcoming but seemingly eager to talk.

"I've been to Fort Davis three times in my twenty-two years of Army service, all within the past six or seven years when we were fighting Comanches," Gerlach said. "Those were the toughest missions I'd had since the Civil War. I hope my combat days are finished, to be honest with you. I never intended to spend my life soldiering. I'm not a West Pointer. I was a high school teacher in Pennsylvania when I signed up for the War of the Rebellion. I thought it was the right and noble thing to do. Well, if there's something noble about war, I haven't found it yet, and, still, here I am. I keep saying I'll go back to teaching when my tour's up, and then I sign on again."

Henry said, "I'm on a scouting mission now to plan a route to bring the Tenth Cavalry Regiment and maybe some infantry from Fort Elliott to Fort Davis."

"Word is that the Buffalo Soldiers are taking over the work of fighting Apache in the Southwest. I guess you're confirming it. We dealt with Comanche and Apache both when I was there. Apache are the worst in my book. They aren't as thick as they were some years back, though. Lots of them have gone to reservations, but there are hold-outs, mostly led by Victorio. He's clever and knows when to make a run for Mexico if the going gets too tough."

"Does he have a large force?"

"It's hard to call the Apache a force as such. They're broken into bands. Sometimes they get together. Victorio is from the Warm Springs band, but sometimes the Mescalero join up with him, and then there's the mix of reservation jumpers that show up for a spell but return to the reservations if they get too hungry. But he can usually put together three hundred or more for a major battle."

"I'm told Fort Davis is pretty much in the middle of it all."

"Davis has been the major combat post down that way for years. It's located at the mouth of a big canyon at the edge of the Davis Mountains and hard to attack from three sides. Since the Civil War, they've had a lot of soldiers stationed there, and the Indians have avoided direct attacks. They wait for detachments to be ordered out from the fort and ambush the troops while on missions. Of course, most of the missions are to chase the Apache out of the area or capture them and take them to the reservation—where many will run off and join up with their bands again."

"Well, can you tell me the best way to get to Fort Davis?"

"I can show you a map in the commandant's office—he's in San Antonio talking to brass right now. You can take some notes from that, if you like. I assume wagons are involved?"

Henry said, "A lot of wagons, maybe some big guns, too."

"Then you will cross the Pecos at Horsehead Crossing."

"And where is that?"

"There is a well-used trail from Concho to the crossing. You will pass through a deep cut in a mesa to reach the crossing—a place called Castle Gap. It's on the old Comanche War Trail. Used to be a lot of travelers ambushed there. Not so likely today. Comanche problem is gone, and the Apache don't generally roam that far north now. Still, you should keep an eye out, and there is some real risk as you get nearer to Fort Davis."

"I have a man with me who has been to Fort Davis. He can tell me more about Horsehead Crossing. Will wagons have a crossing problem?"

"When will you be moving?"

"Late February and early March."

"You should be fine. The river is generally running low that time of year. When you get to late April and into May, you've got to deal with winter thaw from the mountains in New Mexico and Colorado. Anyhow, after you cross the Red River, there will be three possible routes to Fort Davis. I'll show you on the map."

"I would like to bring Sergeant Murphy with me."

"Oh, got you an Irish sergeant, huh?"

Henry smiled. "He's a Buffalo Soldier, but I wouldn't be surprised if he didn't have a bit of Irish in him. He's got the temperament."

"Well, bring him with you. How about right after noon mess? I assume you will join me for officers' mess. Only a half dozen of us here right now."

Chapter 25
Apache Trouble

ENRY WAS WARY when the party rode through the strange slice in the mesa that folks called Castle Gap, he assumed because of the towering knoll near the top of the north side which was covered with huge boulders. Murphy told him the journey through the arroyo was about a mile long, but it seemed like five. He gave a sigh of relief when they broke out of the cut, and he could see ruins of a former Butterfield stage way station abandoned because of Indian assaults and moved to Fort Stockton some thirty-five miles south.

From the hillside above the old station, Henry saw that the river followed a zig-zag course through the semi-arid land, and that the banks were steep and high at most places. The trail, however, led to a portion of the bank that sloped gradually into the river albeit facing a more challenging incline on the southerly side. With the river's present depth, horses should have an easy enough crossing, but moving wagons, although doable, would require care and finesse. The trail revealed that hundreds of wagons and animals had crossed here and broken down the bank considerably.

He dismounted and called Private Stretch Hooper to his side. "Private, you said you've been to Fort Davis before, so I assume you've crossed here before. Is there a better place for wagons to cross the river?"

"No, sir. Ain't nothing unless a feller can add wings. Before spring, they ain't going to get washed away. Just might take some pulling and pushing if some get mired in the mud. Mostly rock along the bottom, though. All the crossers over the years done dug it up some. Heaviest wagons might need an extra team."

"Captain Gerlach helped me come up with a map I've sketched that shows three possible routes to Fort Davis after we cross the Pecos." He pulled a crumpled sheet of paper from his coat pocket, opened it and showed the paper to Hooper. "Have you been on any of these?"

"All of them, sir. This country's mostly rock and gulleys and hills. Desert without much flat if you ask me. Middle trail's the only one you'd get wagons through.

Army always takes its wagons to the fort that way. Is that what we come all this way to decide? I could have told you that back at Elliott."

Henry sighed. Increasingly, he was learning that the Army assigned a lot of wasted missions. He wondered if it was ignorance or a ploy to keep the soldiers busy. He had seen nothing so far that could not have been handled with a few advance scouts like Hooper riding ahead of the contingent. "Well, Private, why don't you take the lead after we cross the river and show us the way to Fort Davis."

"I can do that, sir. Something I was going to mention, though."

"Yes, go ahead."

"I smell Apaches."

"Apache. What do you mean you smell them?"

"Can't explain that, sir, but I know Indians, and I can just tell. Ain't been often wrong. That don't mean they're going to bother us none, but they's watching. We just need to be ready. The fact they're around don't mean they're going to attack us, but I'd bet they got their eyes on some horses and mules, maybe our foodstuffs."

"That's good to know. We'll post a guard with the critters tonight. How many nights to the fort, do you think?"

"Three, if we don't push the critters and pick stops where there's water and some grass yet. Ain't much for horses and mules to eat in the country we're passing through. That's why they used to use camels some down this way."

"Camels? You are serious?"

"Yessir. Never seen any, but I'm told there is still some wild ones about. Army couldn't deal with them. Mean, unruly critters that don't take to training like a horse. Guess some was moved to Arizona but ain't sure how many made it there. I'm guessing they wasn't hitched too tight, and the Army never learned how to hold them in a herd."

"We've been through some rough country. You make this sound worse."

"Let me put it this way. The buffalo hardly ever went south of the Pecos. No good eating down there. That's one reason the Apaches crossed and went north some and got into Comanche territory to hunt. Of course, that didn't go over well with the Comanches, and there was some warring over that."

"But you do know where we can get water and graze the horses?"

"Yessir. Canyons with springs or streams and decent grass for this part of Texas. We can fort up a bit there, too, and hold off an attack if there ain't too many."

"And what if there are too many?"

"Ain't no way out then. One thing, though. It's likely that most of the Apaches have headed south to winter in Mexico. Any left here is likely stragglers, hunting parties maybe making a last hunt. Keep in mind, though, the devils don't mind horsemeat a bit."

The thought of somebody killing and eating his dun stallion, Valiant, sent shivers down his spine. "Thank you, Private. You have been very helpful. You lead the way after we cross the Pecos."

The Pecos crossing was uneventful, but the water was deeper than Henry had anticipated. Fortunately, upon the advice of both Sergeant Milo Murphy and Private Stretch Hooper, the men had removed boots and socks before riding their mounts through the cold water. Henry had been freezing ever since, and a bitter wind had started to sweep across the prairie. It was midafternoon and animals and soldiers were showing some fatigue, and he was relieved when Hooper informed him they should be less than two hours from the first stop.

He was not so pleased when the ex-sergeant added, "And the Apache smell is stronger. They're following us for sure."

Somehow, Henry had confidence in the man's instincts, or at least he was not inclined to bet against it. "Do you think they will hit us before we get to the canyon and set up camp?"

"Not likely. I'm thinking they want to just make off with the horses and mules after we've settled in for the night. But don't count on what I'm guessing. The Apaches survive on surprise."

"I'll warn the men to be alert." His eyes scanned the prairie about him. Rocks scattered everyplace, buttes and small mesas here and there, but he could see nothing that would hide many attackers. Mostly treeless, the area was known as the Chihuahuan Desert that covered parts of northern Mexico and the southwestern United States. It occupied much of West Texas, the lower Pecos Valley in New Mexico, and its fingers even reached into southwestern New Mexico. There were patches of grasses, and he recognized agave, mesquite, yucca and creosote bushes. He wondered why whites even wanted to claim this land.

Henry signaled the riders to a halt and wheeled Valiant to face the men. "Private Hooper says we are less than two hours from our overnight campsite. There is no drinkable water between here and there, so we will keep on moving at our same pace. There is a good spring for watering the horses and resupplying canteens. I must warn you, however, that Private Hooper believes we are being followed by an Apache band. They likely want our horses, but I'm sure they wouldn't turn down an opportunity to harvest some scalps. Keep an eye out and tell me if you see anything suspicious."

He turned back to Hooper. "Private Hooper, how difficult would it be for you get the Apache within your sight and get a count on the size of the party?"

"Easy enough given some time, but I'd have to circle around some. I wouldn't likely return before you get to the canyon where you set up camp."

"Can we find the canyon without you?"

"This old wagon trail passes within a hundred yards of the canyon. You'll come to a big mesa off to your right. You should see a trail where other folks have angled off to the canyon. It's got water, which is hard to come by in these parts. It's a dead-end canyon that goes into the mesa. Go to the far end, and you'll find a stream that comes right out of the wall and goes along the edge of the wall for maybe a hundred feet before it disappears into the wall again. There should be grass down there for the critters. I'd stake them out there and set up camp in front of them. That way, the dang redskins ain't getting the horses without going through us."

That made a certain sense, but there was also no avenue for retreat, which made Henry a bit uneasy. "I'll see how it all looks when we get there. We can change plans, maybe even move on during the night if you find we're badly outnumbered." He reached into his saddle bags, pulled out his telescope, and handed it to the scout. "Take this. It might come in handy."

"Thank you, sir. That just might save my scalp." He gave a quick salute and rode off down the trail in the direction from which they had just come. Sergeant Murphy, who had sidled his mount in next to Henry during the conversation said, "When he's sober, old Stretch generally knows what he's talking about, sir. I've stopped at the canyon with a troop before for water and rest. We won't miss it."

"I wasn't worried about that, Sarge. I'm more concerned about getting trapped there, but we can weigh that better if Private Hooper comes back with some numbers."

"And he will, sir. I'd bet every dollar I've got on that. Of course, I ain't got more than two dollars to last till payday."

Chapter 26
The Raid

WHEN THEY ARRIVED at the canyon, Henry's first thought was that they had come upon an oasis in the middle of a desert. It was a narrow-mouthed canyon, well camouflaged by brush from the main trail's sight. The trail branching off from the route was obviously well-used, and it was unlikely any traveler would miss it. Trees, mostly oak and cottonwood were scattered around the edges of the canyon walls, and he assumed there must be moisture there perhaps seeping out from the stream that was mostly hidden, according to Hooper and Murphy. Most critical for their purposes were the intermittent carpets of browning grass that the horses could graze.

The party entered the canyon which Henry judged to be no more than 150 yards deep and headed toward the far end. He noted that the walls narrowed the farther they went, and he could see that once they set up camp it would be extremely difficult for the Apache to attempt to steal the horses without attacking the soldiers. It was a good place to camp for the night, so he dispatched Corporal Jimmy Mitchell to direct set-up while he and Murphy evaluated defense options.

"Two men should unsaddle the horses and unload the mules and look after them first. We can have a fire tonight. The Indians already know where we're at, so there is no reason to pretend we're hiding. I'll leave it to you to assign the cooking and decide the menu. Split the puptents between the north and south sides of the campsite."

"Yessir, I'll do that."

They surrendered their mounts to one of the privates who would tend to the watering and staking out of animals while Henry and Murphy walked the canyon's perimeter. Henry studied the canyon walls that were separated by no more than a hundred feet at the campsite area. "We need to post two sentries through the night. Two-hour shifts, and you and I will take one so everybody gets some decent sleep."

"Sir, I always heard Apaches are afraid of fighting at night. Dark never kept the Comanches from hitting us."

"I am far from an expert on Indians and their warring habits, Sergeant, but Captain Nolan told me once not to rely on that belief. He said that too many folks have lost their lives by relying upon such notions. As for me, I don't think I would be sleeping anyway."

"Me neither."

Henry pointed to a stone outcropping on the south wall of the canyon. "That will do for this side. A man should be able to climb up there and hunker down some behind the boulders on the edge. With about ten feet off the ground, he would have a good view of anybody coming. No clouds in the sky, so we should get some moonlight."

"Yessir, that looks good. I like the sentry spot. I don't know if I can climb up there myself, though. I got more buffalo than mountain goat in me."

"We'll look for something more accessible on the other side. Private Charlie is heftier than you, and he for sure would have a challenge at this station."

Soon they located another station on the opposite side in a shallow fissure in the canyon wall that provided cover for a sentry. When they returned to camp, Henry was pleased to find that all the puptents were pitched, and the horses were staked out and grazing. Six tents, three on each side of the campsite were lined up, luxury lodging since soldiers often needed to share one of the cramped, A-shaped canvas shelters.

A fire had been started, and it appeared Corporal Mitchell had assumed cooking duties. Since Jimmy was the best cook of the lot, that portended a decent supper. Things happened when he was in charge. Regardless of the corporal's relative youth, Henry would push him to a sergeant's promotion at first opportunity. He hoped that not many years would pass before non-academy soldiers like Jimmy Mitchell might find opportunities within commissioned ranks.

"Rider coming," Murphy said. "I think it's Stretch."

Henry turned back to the canyon's mouth and saw the horse and rider, half hidden in a dust cloud, moving their direction. He watched and waited, confirming that it was indeed the lanky Private Hooper and walked out to greet him.

Hooper reined in and dismounted, offering a sloppy salute as Henry approached. "Lieutenant, sir, I found them Apaches. They ain't more than a few miles from here, but they know where we're at. It ain't a question no more of 'if.' It's just 'when,' and they ain't likely planning to follow us all the way to Fort Davis. I'd say they'll hit tonight or in the morning, maybe right after sunrise."

"How many?"

He returned Henry's telescope. "Thanks to this here spyglass, I got a good count. There's nine. They got some rifles amongst them, but most can't hit much if they ain't up close. No match for us on direct attack. They might go for ambush, but they'd rather snatch some horses and run for it."

"We've staked the horses between our campsite and the canyon walls. I'm putting out sentries tonight, so they can't reach the horses without coming through us."

"I don't think it's likely the whole party would come this far into the canyon. They'd send two or three with the notion of running off the horses, and then they'd catch as many as they could at the canyon's mouth."

"So we had best be looking for something to happen tonight?"

"Feller never knows, but that's they way I see it, sir."

"Early or late?"

"I'd say early. Why would they wait? I'd want to get my horses and disappear into the dark. Even if they got just a few of our critters, would we be trying to chase them down in the dark?"

Henry said, "You did a good job, Corporal, and I appreciate the benefit of your experience."

"Don't suppose I could get a few corporal's stripes out of this. I'd like to start working my way back up."

Henry smiled. He liked this guy, and he had been a treasure trove of information. "I'll do what I can, but tonight you and I are going to take first watch."

"Yessir. I think it's the best chance for some fun."

Henry did not anticipate fun, but he did want to acquire the experience of Apache confrontation.

After a supper of bacon and beans and apple cobbler, Henry spoke to his soldiers. "Pair up for two-hour watches tonight. I've shown you the sentry posts. Sleep with uniforms and boots on and weapons within reach. If you hear a gunshot, get out fast and get to the horses. If Apache hit, they're likely after the horses. Unless you want to walk to Fort Davis, we can't let them get away with the animals. Fire at will if you see one of the raiders."

After the sun disappeared over the canyon rim, Henry and Hooper claimed their sentry posts, Henry opting for the one atop the stone outcropping, so he would have a view of most of the canyon. Little more than an hour later, he saw movement not more than a hundred feet distant. It was a man creeping through the trees along the canyon wall. How did he get so near without being spotted?

And there were likely others. They would not have sent a single warrior. Of course, he could be scouting out locations before they decided how to make their move. He looked across the canyon and caught sight of movement near Hooper's post, two men merely dancing shadows in the moonlight from his distance. They were entangled, engaged in combat. He thought of the non-regulation Bowie knife sheathed on Hooper's belt. He must have taken on the Apache hand-to-hand to maintain the quiet for a spell. Now there was a single shadow standing.

He turned his attention back to the Apache on his side of the canyon. He had crept to within fifty feet now. Henry had not brought his sword, thinking it was too cumbersome. It also had a way of striking obstructions as it swung on his waist, risking the possibility of disclosing the wearer's whereabouts. The warrior would see or hear him if he moved, and he feared that he was a better target on his perch than the Apache was weaving through the trees and undergrowth. He decided to attract the stalker's attention on his own terms.

He rose up and groaned before half sliding and half tumbling down the slope that led to the overhang, clutching his rifle in one hand and pistol in the other. When he struck the canyon floor, he lay still, stretched on the ground and feigning injury. His rifle was tossed off to the side but his Colt remained grasped in his hand. His plan was to draw the warrior to him and to surprise the attacker with a lead slug to his chest.

He had not counted on the visitor's speed, however, because before he could orient himself, fingers closed around his throat and a knee drove into his groin sending excruciating pain and a wave of nausea through his body. His fingers released their hold on the Colt, and it dropped on the ground beside him. Henry looked up and saw an angry face with hate-filled eyes and his free hand holding an upraised war axe ready to arc down and split his foe's skull.

The warrior, evidently confident Henry was disabled, released his hold on the throat, and Henry lunged away just as the war axe drove past his head. He felt the burn of the axe's blade but did not have time to give it a thought. He rolled now, tossing the warrior off him. Frantically, he sought his pistol, seeing that his would-be assailant was back on his feet with axe upraised, ready to pounce again. He grasped the pistol, feeling like it was taking valuable minutes to raise and ready to fire.

He heard the crack of rifle fire nearby but ignored it. The warrior looked away briefly, obviously distracted by the sound. By the time he turned back to Henry, the soldier was squeezing the trigger of his own weapon and planting two lead slugs in his chest. The war axe slipped from his hand, and he followed the weapon to the earth.

"Lieutenant, Lieutenant. You alright, sir?" It was Sergeant Milo Murphy's voice.

His response was delayed by the sound of more gunfire, lots of it. When the racket seemed to move toward the mouth of the canyon, he yelled, "Over here, Sergeant. I'm alright."

Shortly, Murphy crashed through the surrounding brush. "Didn't know what become of you, sir. You wasn't up there at your post."

"Well, I had a tussle with this fellow on the ground, and it was more luck than skill or brains that I'm alive. What's happening?"

"Old lady luck was with all of us, I'd say. Jimmy went out to take a piss, and he saw Stretch taking an Apache warrior down, and he come and woke me up. We figured we'd best roust the others and be ready. Lots of reasons that warning gunshot might not go off. Stretch saw us and come running over and says the whole damn bunch of redskins was moving in, following back a ways. Guess they decided to collect some scalps while they was stealing horses. We couldn't see you, because you was hidden from the campsite by the trees."

"I take it the Apache are on the run?"

"Yessir, we was ready by the time the main body moved up. I left Jimmy and Stretch in charge while I headed over to check on you. Danged if I didn't see one of the devils headed your way, and I took him down back there, and I guess that got everybody shooting. Anyhow the gunfire was all moving in the right direction, so I don't think them Injuns will be pestering us no more."

"Well, let's get back to the camp and see what's happening."

"Lieutenant, sir. I think you got blood running down your head and neck, just behind the right ear."

Henry pressed his fingers to the side of his head and felt the sticky mess. "I guess the war axe got a piece of my head, but it doesn't appear he split my head wide open."

Murphy moved nearer and placed this hand on Henry's head. "Nasty cut, it looks like. Likely needs some stitching. I think there's a needle and thread of some kind in the first aid box the quartermaster put together. Likely gauze and patching tape, too."

"Maybe we can tape a compress on till we get to Fort Davis. They should have a few surgeons there."

"That's true enough, but we're a few days away. Not stepping on your rank, sir, but I'm thinking you ought to get it done now. Heal better and less chance of putrefaction of some sort. We can get a better look under a lantern when we get back to camp. Can you walk that far?"

"Walking's no problem, but who's going to do the sewing?"

"I can do it, sir. Until I was assigned to a colored outfit, I served as a unofficial medic during the War of the Rebellion. During slave days, I worked on horses and cows and such, and when the Union Army freed us, some of us went along to do chores of sorts. At first, I did horses, but when they got short of surgeons, I got shifted to soldiers."

"We'll give it a try." He took several steps toward the camp, and that was the last thing he remembered. He was confused when he awakened stretched out near the campfire on his bedroll, the glare of a lantern above his head nearly blinding him. For a few moments he was uncertain where he was.

Murphy gently pulled him back to his mission, waving the holder of the lantern back and kneeling over him. "You keeled over, sir, and have been out a spell. Worked out fine. I put about ten stitches in your head, cleaned up the wound. Deeper than I guessed, but you should heal up fine. Likely have a scar to remember the night by."

Henry's hand went to the side of his head where he could feel the compress anchored by a strip of cloth wrapped around the head and knotted at the base of his skull. "Thank you, Sergeant, for looking after me. The men . . . anybody injured?

"Nary a scratch. Can't say as much for them Apaches. Four dead, at least two wounded, maybe more. We got the mules out and got them hauling bodies out to the canyon mouth. Stretch says they'll be gone by the time we leave in the morning. Apaches ain't inclined to leave their dead behind, and they still had their horses tied someplace. We're done with that bunch. Just as soon not run into any others before we get to Fort Davis."

"It sounds like you've got everything in order, Sergeant. I fear I won't be much help for a spell. I want to pull out in the morning even if you've got to tie me to my stallion."

Henry dropped off to sleep again but opened his eyes to the smell of biscuits, bacon, and coffee. Somehow, he had ended up in his puptent. He supposed that was Murphy's doing. He struggled some to get free of the blankets and then crawled out of the tent. This time, the source of the light that blinded him was a bright sun creeping over the east canyon wall.

Corporal Jimmy Mitchell was kneeling near the fire, lifting the lid of the Dutch oven that sat on some coals that had been scraped off to one side. When Henry was out of the tent, he struggled to his feet and almost dropped to the ground again when dizziness struck him. He stood for a bit, and his head began to clear.

"Good morning, Lieutenant. Biscuits will be ready in a few minutes. I'll get you a mug of hot coffee and have a tin plate with bacon and biscuits shortly. Maybe if you get a bite to eat, that will perk you up some." He pointed to a big, half-rotted log. "Sarge had a few of the guys roll that log in there. He thought maybe you'd like to sit on it."

The men were spoiling him, but he was not about to decline the help just now. He took tentative steps to the log and let himself down. A few minutes later, the corporal presented the cup of coffee, and a few sips started to bring him back to life. He was suddenly starving and when the breakfast plate appeared, he devoured the contents and accepted the offer of a second biscuit. When he was finished, and the men began to straggle in from whatever chores Murphy had assigned, he was confident he would not need to be tied to his mount when they broke camp and rode out of the canyon.

Chapter 27
Jordy

I WAS ON ANOTHER wasted Apache mission the first time Henry and his scouting party showed up at Fort Davis, but my lady friend told me about his visit. She even met him and tended to an injury that had already been well cared for by a sergeant. She raved about how handsome and well-spoken Lieutenant Flipper was, and I have got to admit it aggravated me some. I hoped that Henry would stand away from offering amorous competition for a longtime friend.

You see, Taryn Blair was a contract surgeon for Fort Davis. One of the few female physicians in the West. For that matter, there would not have been many anyplace in the country. The Army was desperate for doctors, so they were taking on civilians as contract surgeons and paid them better than a captain's salary. Nobody wanted to come to Fort Davis. It was an isolated place in a barren land, and worst of all still engaged in the Apache wars.

Taryn liked adventure. Why in blazes she suffered me, I will never understand. I avoid adventure when I can. Anyhow, Taryn was a beautiful creature with auburn hair and jade-green eyes and a sprinkling of freckles across her nose that faded away onto her cheeks. She was a lithe, tall woman just a few inches shorter than my six feet, a bit small-breasted for some maybe, but decent curves in the right places. She turned a lot of eyes on the post, that's for sure.

I had only seen Dr. Taryn Blair from a distance until I visited the post hospital the previous fall. I had put treatment of my ailment off too long and would not be able to sit a horse much longer. There were three surgeons on the post at the time, one extra because of anticipation of the Tenth joining us soon for an all-out assault on the Apache. We were assigned to a surgeon and had no input in the selection. Well, I suspect a prank, but I was assigned to Dr. Blair. That would have been fine, but I was suffering from a huge abscess on my skinny ass. I was not enthusiastic about seeing a female doctor.

I met Taryn for the first time in the surgery, very intimate, just the two of us. I explained my problem, and she maintained a straight face and showed appropriate concern. I was shaking when she told me to remove my britches and undershorts and get up on the surgery table, belly down, but I could not accomplish this without revealing all my private parts. I swear my pizzle shrank to grubworm size that morning, and I figured I wasn't making an impression, but at least she wasn't laughing out loud.

Anyhow, I obeyed, and Taryn examined the abscess, probing with fingers that seemed none too gentle. She asked, "Painful?"

"Yes, doctor. Very."

"I don't see how you can sit a horse."

"It's not fun."

The next thing I know, I've got pus and blood running all over my ass. She had taken a scalpel and opened the dang thing without warning. Now she was squeezing the smelly mess out, and it just kept coming. The pain, though, wasn't all that bad in comparison to sitting on the darned abscess.

She said, "A wood tick started all this trouble. You've had this a long time, haven't you? You just kept scratching and digging at it till it got worse, probably helped the infection along."

"I can't deny it."

"Well, next time get in here as soon as the problem comes up, and I'll give it early attention. There is no sense in suffering the way you have. Now I'll get a wet cloth and clean you up and put some salve and a loose compress on the wound. I want it to drain, and it's okay if you press around the wound to encourage drainage. I want you back here in three days, so I can see how it's coming along. I don't want to reopen it unless the swelling's not going down. I will issue an order that you are not to ride a horse until I give you a release."

Well, she washed off my buttocks and thighs with gentle hands, and when I walked out of her office, I was in love. She later told me she thought I behaved like a school child when I was seeing her. I did not cry, but I admit I don't like visiting doctors generally. In fact, I fear them and expect a death sentence whenever I submit to one.

I must return to Henry's story. Fort Davis came alive when the Tenth Cavalry arrived along with two infantry companies, one white and the other colored. We did not have sufficient barracks, and many of the newcomers had to continue camping in their tents. The fort fronts a canyon in the low Davis Mountains and the semi-arid surrounding hills and plains which contrast sharply with the large canyon's water, trees and grass making it a virtual oasis in a vast desert.

Henry and I greeted each other with a firm handshake and quick embrace. I was glad to see him, but happier still to see that Captain Nicholas Nolan and his family, including Mollie Dwyer, were a part of the contingent. Assuming Mollie and Henry were still inviting scandal, he would not be pursuing Taryn, and I suspected she would not be put off by his color. I vowed to tell him about my tentative, clumsy courting of Taryn at first opportunity.

It was a week before we had a chance to talk at length in Henry's quarters which were no longer a part of the Nolan household. "What do you think of Fort Davis?" I asked as we sat at his kitchen table.

"Frankly, I miss Fort Sill. I got attached to that place, but this will grow on me, and I need to see more combat to have any hope for future promotion."

We talked for well over an hour about our experiences during the period we had been separated, but my curiosity finally got the best of me. "Flip, you're not lodging with the Nolans here."

"Yeah, they have a smaller house at Davis. Besides, I spoke with the captain and suggested that in light of rumors about Mollie and me, it might be best if I occupied my own officer's quarters. I think he might have been relieved some."

I played dumb. "Rumors about you and Mollie? What are you talking about?"

"We go riding together quite frequently, and then my rooming in the same house. It's bound to cause talk. Some folks no doubt disapprove of any kind of relationship between a colored man and white woman. I don't want to cause any embarrassment for the family. They're wonderful people. Besides, I'm ready for a little privacy."

"Then you won't be seeing Mollie anymore?"

"I never was 'seeing her' in the way you're thinking. We are friends, and she still insists that I will take her riding."

"No romance in your future then?"

"To be honest, I would like that to happen, but I just don't know. What about you? Any romance on your agenda?"

I told him about Dr. Taryn Blair, including the story of our first meeting. Flip did not laugh easily, but he loosened up with that tale. "Taryn is about three years older than I am, almost twenty-seven, she said, and I already felt like a boy at first. But I finally got up the nerve to ask her to dance at a post July 4 celebration, and we ended up sharing most of the dances that night. That gave me the gumption to ask her to the August dance—there is a post-wide dance monthly. No officers' ball but whites and colored folks all attend. There are only a few of the Buffalo sergeants and corporals who have wives here, but there are a lot of colored women doing cleaning and laundry with their eyes open for prospective mates."

"The dances aren't segregated then?"

"Well, no, but I've never seen whites and coloreds paired up in a dance."

"I'm not much of a dancer anyhow."

I could see that Flip's attraction to Mollie was more than friendship. I suspected he loved that woman. I understood now that I had come to care for Taryn. We were having dinner Saturday evenings at her quarters by that time, her living arrangements being much nicer than mine. We shared her bed those nights until just before sunrise, and I like to think she got over what was likely her first impression of my equipment. Anyway, she never mentioned it, and she kept inviting me back. I had marriage on my mind now but was not yet comfortable broaching the subject. It was all so complicated with my years of military service remaining.

I shared none of this with Flip, of course, given his own dilemma. Regardless, it was good to be with the man I respected more than any other again.

Chapter 28
New Assignments

FTER HIS RESCUE of Colonel Benjamin Grierson and his besieged party, Henry always seemed to rise to the top of the list when the colonel was selecting officers for special assignments. He welcomed work in the field and the opportunities to make a mark that might lead to future promotions, increasingly hard to come by in the post-Civil War Army. His assignments, however, sometimes drew resentment from other officers, especially that of his new first lieutenant, Charles E. Nordstrom.

Henry had not previously endured significant slights or blatant discrimination during his Army service, and he had never given much thought to such things, focusing only on doing his very best at whatever task was placed in his lap. Nordstrom, outranking Henry, never hesitated to complain when he was passed over for some mission assigned by Colonel Grierson and more than once suggested to Henry that Grierson was catering to his color. Henry once overheard Nordstrom speaking to another officer and referring to him as the "colonel's pet nigger." That had been one of the few occasions Henry had nearly lost control of his temper, but as usual he thought ahead and considered the consequences of a confrontation and possible fisticuffs.

What stung worse was the gradual tapering of his horseback rides with Mollie Dwyer. Since Nordstrom's arrival, she no longer asked him to take her for rides, and more recently she had started declining his invitations. And now, she was spending nice Sunday afternoons riding with Nordstrom in his buggy.

It was clear that Nordstrom was seriously courting Mollie and twice now Nordstrom had also been a guest when Annie Nolan invited Henry to an occasional Sunday dinner. After the awkwardness of the third such occasion, Henry always found an assignment he had to tend to when an invitation came his way. Finally, the invitations ceased. He knew that Annie was in an awkward position and understood. She was probably relieved to reduce the unavoidable tension at Sunday dinners.

His relationship with Captain Nolan was unaffected, and he appreciated that Nolan tried to separate the first and second lieutenants as often as possible but given that Henry was junior to Nordstrom that was not always feasible. It did not help that Henry and Nordstrom shared double quarters. The arrangement included a common entrance and hall, but otherwise quarters were separate. It was rare that a day passed that the two men did not encounter each other in entering or exiting their lodging places, however.

This morning, Henry was waiting in the office of Major N.B. McLaughlin, Fort Davis's commanding officer. Although outranked by Colonel Grierson, McLaughlin oversaw the administration of the post, and Grierson's responsibilities were to command the Ninth and Tenth Buffalo Soldiers and conduct the war effort. Henry liked McLaughlin. The major was a kind and gentle sort and had visited him daily for nearly a week during his bout with malaria a month earlier. He had no idea why he had been summoned.

When the desk sergeant escorted him into the major's office, after the perfunctory salutes and formalities, the major stepped out from behind his desk and gripped Henry's hand, pumping it enthusiastically. "Wonderful to see you on your feet again, Lieutenant. Sit down, I have two things to discuss with you."

Henry took the chair in front of the desk and faced the middle-aged officer, whose twinkling blue eyes seemed to be evaluating him. McLaughlin was a full-bearded man with dark brown hair, trim and fit, unlike some senior officers, and spoke with a soft voice that beckoned a man to listen carefully.

The major said, "I stated I had two matters to discuss. Colonel Grierson assured me that you are a man I can count on, and I have seen nothing to contradict his opinion. As you know, most of the men are in the field a hundred or so miles to the south and west, chasing Victorio and his darned Apache. That's where you would be if the malaria hadn't hit you. I want you to join them now."

"Gladly, sir."

"You will not be engaged in serious fighting, or at least that is not the intent of your mission. You are going to be a courier. I have a message from Washington to call in the troops. There is to be a truce with Apache while an emissary from Arizona meets with Victorio. I am sending an officer, so Colonel Grierson will understand the importance of his return. I daresay he will not be pleased with the order. I will have a written message that recites the Washington order, but I want you to tell him of our conversation."

"I can do that, but I don't understand what I should tell him, sir."

"Mister Flipper, I wish you to explain my reluctance to deliver this order but to stress that that this comes directly from President Rutheford Hayes. His term will end soon, and he wants to see the conflict with the Apache ended before he leaves office next March. The Indian problems have been very much on his mind. I will refrain from expressing my thoughts on this, but I want you to emphasize to the colonel that I want his troops called in judiciously, so we don't have unnecessary casualties. Hayes is not seeking re-election, so I suspect troops will remain at Fort Davis until after the election, which is only a few months away. Garfield or Hancock will determine the course of the Indian wars after that."

Hayes was a Republican, and Henry had voted for him. He generally agreed with the President's suspicion of the reservation system and his proposals that encouraged assimilation, but they appeared to be going nowhere. He would doubtless vote for Republican Garfield, but the candidate had been vague about Indian issues. He supposed that Hayes was hampered by his personal unpopularity and the fact that although he had narrowly won the electoral vote, he had decisively lost the popular vote.

"I will convey your thoughts about the implementation of the orders, sir, but, of course, I am a soldier of much lesser rank."

"He respects you, Lieutenant. He has told me as much, and you may emphasize that you are only conveying my wishes that the orders be carried out in the manner he deems prudent."

"Yessir."

"Now, there is the other matter. Our post quartermaster will be leaving next month for another assignment, and before they departed for the battlefield, I asked both Captain Nolan and Colonel Grierson if they might provide me with a list of men who might temporarily fill that position. You were first named by both. When you return, I am ordering you to assume the quartermaster's responsibilities until otherwise filled."

Henry was not excited about this development. "Sir, if that is your wish, I will, of course, do so, but I have no experience."

"You can read and write, and I am informed you are exceptionally good with numbers. That narrows the field considerably. I will see that you have the assistance you require, and I have no doubt you will grasp the procedures in little time at all. I anticipate you will master the job quickly."

"Yessir."

Flipper was to depart for the Rio Grande the next morning, and Major McLaughlin hoped he might locate Colonel Grierson in two days' time. He would ride his stallion, Valiant, and take a spare mount for alternating. A pack horse would slow him, so he would pack survival rations and necessities in the saddle bags on the two mounts. The route that the Army had taken south would have water sources. He wondered how he would find Colonel Grierson after he reached the Rio Grande.

Before he left, he wanted to speak to two women. First stop was Dr. Taryn Blair, and he checked at the post hospital to see if she was free. The other two surgeons had gone with the troops, but as a woman she had been left behind to tend to those remaining at the post. She had looked after him during his illness, and a friendship had developed to the point that she did not hesitate to complain about her abandonment. She had wanted to go with the troops.

He found her free at the hospital, and they spoke in her closet-sized office. "I wasn't sure I would have an opportunity to speak with you before I rode out, but I just wanted to thank you for the care you gave me when I was ill. I know some thought I would die."

She smiled, crinkling her nose as she often did. "There is not much chance I wouldn't be able to talk. I have little to do with most of the troops gone. As to your care, Jordy would never have forgiven me if I let his best friend die."

"Well, doctor . . ."

"Taryn. I assume this is not a professional visit."

He said, "No. I just wanted you to know I am leaving to join the troops and expect to bring Jordy and the others back with me. I suspect you will soon have plenty of business again."

"I will be glad to have him back. I'm sure you have figured it out, but I love that guy."

"I know, and the feeling is mutual."

"He's never told me so."

"Jordy's shy and not always confident, but when the going gets rough, you can count on him. I don't know a better man, but he tends to underestimate his abilities."

"What do you think he would say if I asked him to marry me?"

She caught him totally off guard with that question. "He would say 'yes.'"

"I'm tired of waiting, and I'm not getting any younger. I'm twenty-seven years old, you know, almost three years older than you and Jordy."

"That hardly makes you an old woman, and most men would guess you to be not yet twenty."

"Jordy warned me to watch out for you, that you had a way with women."

"Not all, I'm afraid. My next visit is with Mollie Dwyer."

"She is a delightful young woman, but I am not unaware of the talk that you haven't been seeing her so much lately."

"No, I haven't. She has been spending a lot of time with Lieutenant Nordstrom. I have never spoken of this to anyone else, but I think she cares for me—or did— but cannot cross the invisible line between colored and white."

"I am sorry, Henry. I truly am. For what it is worth, if I had not met Jordy first, I would have had my eyes on you and would have been able to cross that line. There is someone out there for you, white or colored. You have time. Be patient."

He got up to leave, and Taryn stepped around her desk and gave him a hug and soft kiss on the cheek. "Hurry back and bring that crazy Jordy Dixon with you."

He went to the Nolan house, and when he rapped on the door, Mollie answered. She stepped out to speak with him, and he suspected Annie was within hearing distance in the house. It occurred to him only then that he did not know precisely why he had made this visit.

They stood on the porch silently, a respectful distance from each other, as always, aware that the eyes of post occupants would be watching and creating daily gossip. "I just wanted to let you know that I will be heading south as a courier to the troops tomorrow. Major McLaughlin said my message was no secret, and that he would be informing wives and families later today. The cavalry and infantry regiments have been ordered back to Fort Davis. You might wish to tell Annie that the captain will be home soon."

"Oh, that's very kind of you, Henry. Annie and the kids will be so excited."

"I just thought you might like to know. I guess that's all I had to say."

"Henry, there is something I should tell you."

"Yes?"

"I am going to be married soon. I have accepted Charles Nordstrom's proposal of marriage."

He hesitated for a moment, not quite certain how to react. "I wish you both the very best. Lieutenant Nordstrom is a very lucky man."

Chapter 29
The Interpreter

THE RIDE TO the Rio Grande was more challenging than Henry expected. It was late summer now and the torrid afternoon sun still baked the Chihuahuan Desert lands and by afternoon became the enemy of man and horses. The first day out, he quickly decided that he would rest the horses at the first water hole he found after the sun was highest and then ride into the night.

The trail was easy enough to follow, the troops and supply wagons marking the landscape with signs of their passage. He had never seen so much horse dung scattered across the prairie. He kept his eyes open for Apache signs but saw nothing until the morning of the second day when he passed a half dozen horse skeletons picked clean by scavengers now. A few arrows near the remains suggested the animals were killed by Indians, so there must have been an attack of some sort.

He could not imagine the Apache having a force large enough to take on the main body of soldiers, but he knew that war parties sometimes made quick strikes at the rear of columns and then retreated before the enemy could reorganize and turn to fight. Apache were especially adept at—and seemed to prefer—skirmishes and small battles where they could deplete an enemy's force a bit at a time.

He arrived at the Rio Grande early morning following his second night of riding. Small encampments of soldiers lined the river both upstream and downstream every hundred yards or so for as far as he could see, campfire smoke revealing the camps hidden by distance or the river's twists and turns.

He reined Valiant toward some familiar faces from his own Tenth Cavalry, leading the sorrel gelding behind him. Corporal Jimmy Mitchell saw him first and hollered, "Lieutenant, sir. Just in time for breakfast. Come right on over. You look like a man that could eat biscuits and bacon and maybe enjoy a mug of coffee."

"You read my mind, Corporal." He dismounted.

Mitchell called to one of the men, "Private Danner. Tend to the lieutenant's horses and put them on the grass with the remuda."

As soon as the private led the horses away, the corporal handed Henry a tin mug of steaming hot coffee. "No table and chairs, sir, but you can sit on that horse blanket next to the cottonwood over there. Lean back some against the trunk. Might feel good after your saddle time. I'll bring you a plate in a few minutes."

"You're spoiling me, Corporal," Henry said when Jimmy brought him a plate. "I'm near starving, and I do appreciate it."

"My pleasure, Lieutenant. I'm just mighty glad to see you're back on your feet. Word was that you were a mighty sick man when the regiment left Fort Davis."

"I'm fine now, but I need to get a message to Colonel Grierson as soon as possible. Any idea where he can be found?"

"Yessir. Less than a mile upstream. I heard he will be meeting with some brass from the Mexican Army this afternoon. They're crossing the river to palaver with him."

"After I eat, I'd better head up that way. The colonel might want to see my message before he talks with those gentlemen. Have we lost any men in our regiment? I saw signs of fighting along the trail."

"Nobody in the Tenth's got as much as a scratch, but the Ninth has been hit hard. We've been lined up along the river for a good week, not sure why, but the Ninth has been out trying to chase Apaches down, without much luck from what I hear. The devils either disappear or come at you from out of nowhere. Lost two men and a half dozen wounded that the docs are dealing with out of a couple of big tents set up near Colonel Grierson's headquarters upriver. And then we got a missing patrol of about ten men. They was supposed to return in a day. Been gone three days now. Not looking good."

"That's not good. Who's the officer with the patrol?"

"Oh, Lordy, sir. I forgot till now. He's a friend of yours. Lieutenant Jordan Dixon."

Henry felt like he had been slugged in the gut, and if he had not finished eating, he would have lost his appetite. Jordy was the only truly close friend he had in this world. Jordy was his brother. He knew Jordy far better than his flesh and blood brothers.

"What was their mission, do you know?"

"Patrols have all been trying to find out where the Apaches are at. I ain't figured out what good that does, since they'll be fifty miles from where they were seen if soldiers go back. I suppose there's a purpose. Who am I to question strategies and orders?"

"I need to get my message to the colonel."

"Let your critters rest, sir. I'll fetch my gelding. He ain't had any work for a week."

"Thank you, Corporal. I'll take you up on that."

An hour later, Henry rode into the commanding officer's encampment. He hitched his mount to a crude hitching rail not far from the command tent, which consisted of two wall tents spliced together. The colonel enjoyed the luxury of a fragile-appearing cot that lifted the occupant no more than a foot off the ground. He sat on a crude stool lashed from wood harvested from trees along the river and was bent over a metal folding table that was no more than three by three feet. Two similar stools were positioned near the table.

The colonel seemed absorbed with some papers in front of him and had a worried look on his face. Henry cleared his throat, and the colonel looked up.

"Lieutenant Flipper. This is a surprise. So good to see you are still among us."

Henry saluted. "Yessir, I'm glad, too. I bring a message from Major McLaughlin."

"Well, sit down while I take a look at it."

Henry handed him the sealed envelope and sat down on one of the wobbly stools that gave him little confidence in its stability.

Colonel Grierson opened the envelope and removed the sheet of parchment. He read the short message and sighed, setting it aside. "You are aware of the contents?"

"I haven't read the message, Colonel, but the Major told me the gist of it."

"I am to return to Fort Davis with the troops 'as soon as reasonably possible.' At least he has cut me a little slack."

"I don't understand, sir."

"He used some weasel words. 'As soon as reasonably possible.' Not 'instantly' or 'forthwith.' We must withdraw soon, but we likely are being granted several days, certainly no more than a week, to advance the mission."

"I see." But he did not. To Henry, orders were orders and must be obeyed to the letter; however, perhaps the colonel was teaching him about the prerogatives of the higher-ranking officers and the code with which some communicated. He started to rise. "Is there anything else, sir?"

"Not unless you can read Spanish."

"Uh, I do read Spanish, sir."

Grierson brightened. "You do?"

"Yessir."

"We received this from a Mexican soldier who crossed the Rio Grande last night. My meeting with the Mexican general had already been scheduled. Neither Captain Nolan nor Lieutenant Nordstrom can read a word of Spanish, and I asked them to pass the word that we are looking for an interpreter. You arrived just in time." He pushed three sheets of paper across the table. "I don't want a word for word translation. Just take a few minutes to read it and summarize what it says."

Henry read the message which was handwritten in beautiful script. It was essentially an outline of a proposal from a Mexican general. "It's a proposed plan from General Arturo Chavez."

"I could make out the general's name. He is the one I will be meeting with."

"He explains that he will be discussing with you a plan to drive Victorio and his band across the Rio Grande to the Mexican side of the border. He has located the mountain sanctuary that the Apache will retreat to and has a large force of soldiers ready to entrap the warriors as soon as they settle in their hideaway in the illusion that they are safe. He wants your Army to make a sweep that will funnel the Apache to a particular crossing."

"We cannot catch them all in such a sweep."

"He states that he only wants Victorio and the warriors in his party. He insists that when the others learn that Victorio has gone to the sanctuary, the others will follow."

"That makes a certain sense. We just want the Apache out of the United States if they won't surrender, but I would need to accomplish this in three or four-days' time. I must return with the troops to Fort Davis soon, but if I can help bring an end to this scourge, I will have done my duty."

Henry saw an opportunity. "Sir, may I share my thoughts about this?"

"Certainly Lieutenant Flipper. Go right ahead."

"I originally reported here with the thought that I would request your permission to take a half dozen men to seek out the fate of the missing patrol. I would take Sergeant Milo Murphy, Corporal Jimmy Mitchell, and four privates who accompanied me on a scouting trip to Fort Davis. That would include Private Stretch Hooper who had considerable experience during the Red River War against the Comanche. While seeking the lost patrol, we would attempt to locate Victorio. If we do that, I would order Hooper to keep the chief in sight. Another man would remain with him to bring word back on whatever day you designate the troops to move on the Apache."

"Mister Flipper, I think that is an excellent idea. You may collect the men who will join you, and if any officer questions what you are doing, inform him that I have ordered your action. There is only one proviso."

"Yessir?"

"You will return here at one o'clock to act as my inter-preter when the Mexican General and his staff cross the river. I may have more explicit orders after that meeting."

"I will be here, sir."

Chapter 30
Searching For Jordy

THE MEN HAD ridden together for many days on their previous scouting trip, and it made for a more relaxed mission. Each knew how the others would react in given situations, and regardless of rank, the informal pecking order with respect to camp tasks, such as cooking, horse care and other routines took over.

Henry had enjoyed his interpreting task when the Mexican general and his aides arrived. He always welcomed opportunities to speak Spanish to some of the reservation Indians who knew more Spanish from trading with Mexicans than English. There was a significant Mexican population in the Fort Davis civilian community adjacent to the post, including several business owners. He had found practical use for his Spanish language skills in the Southwest. He suspected his French fluency would gradually slip away from lack of use, but one never knew what was around the next corner.

His greatest satisfaction at the meeting between Colonel Grierson and General Chavez had been the obvious annoyance of Lieutenant Nordstrom at the interpreter's role in the proceedings. Captain Nolan, of course, had been his usual congenial self and even offered to assign more men to the search mission if Henry needed them. Henry declined, thinking that a small party would maneuver more successfully on a scouting mission.

The party moved northwest from the Rio Grande, Stretch roaming a good mile ahead of the others. On the first afternoon they rode no more than ten miles from the main encampment, but midmorning of the second, Henry saw the dust cloud when Stretch headed back their way. From the speed the scout was moving, Henry knew important news was coming. He signaled his men to a halt, and they waited for Stretch's arrival.

Soon Stretch rode up, reining his mount in just in front of Henry. "Big trouble three or four miles up ahead, Lieutenant. Apaches got some soldiers cornered in an arroyo. I sighted in with your spyglass from a hilltop. Apaches don't seem to be in no hurry. I'm guessing they've had the soldiers cornered a spell."

"How many soldiers?"

"Maybe three standing upright with rifle barrels propped on the arroyo rim. Appeared to be another wounded and at least three others dead I'm guessing, drug down the wash aways."

"And the Apache?"

"Maybe a dozen. They ain't mounted. They got their horses staked along with at least four cavalry mounts behind a butte maybe fifty yards back. Soldiers ain't got horses. There are a few dead ones laying not far from the arroyo. What the Apaches didn't steal, I'm guessing they run off. Soldiers ain't going no place. No water. Apaches are just wearing them down some before they run them over. Probably give them a taste of some of the afternoon sun before they make their final attack."

"With soldiers in the country, I wouldn't expect them to wait another night. How close can we get before the Apache spot us?"

"Hilly in these parts. We got decent cover, so I'm thinking we could get within a few hundred yards."

"How hard would it be to run off the Apache horses and grab a few of the Army horses?"

Stretch said, "They likely got one guard. I'd have to take him out. If we're going to capture a few critters, I'd need another man. Private Landry is good with horses.

I fire a shot at the guard, though, and it will bring the other devils running."

"What if you don't make your move till we start shooting?"

"My shot would just mix in with the others. You ain't going to charge them? There's just five of you. Asking your pardon, sir. It ain't my place . . ."

"It's alright, Private. There are also the men in the arroyo. Hopefully, they'll catch on and pitch in. We aren't going to try to overrun a dozen Apache. When we get within range, we'll dismount and commence firing. I want you to drive those horses out where the Apache will see them. I'm betting that will get their attention."

"I understand, sir. We can do that."

Fifteen minutes later, Stretch and Private Landry split off while Henry and his party continued their way through the hills. He could hear sporadic gunfire as they neared.

Sergeant Milo Murphy rode beside him now along with Corporal Jimmy Mitchell, the two privates and a packhorse following behind. "What do you make of the gunfire, Sarge?"

"Ain't serious. They're just letting each other know they're ready for a fight."

"From what Stretch said, I don't think our men are that ready."

"They're Buffalo Soldiers, sir. They ain't afraid, and they ain't going down easy without taking company along."

Henry appreciated Murphy's pride in the colored soldiers, and he shared that pride. They were quickly gaining a reputation as the best fighting men in the U.S. Army. "Hopefully, we're not losing any more men today."

Another half hour later the Apache warriors and trapped soldiers came within his sight. He signaled a halt. "We're going to charge those Apache, but when I signal halt, rein in the horses and dismount. After you stake the animals, line up beside me about ten paces apart, rifles at the ready. When I say 'fire,' pick your target and fire at will. We should be within easy range."

They rode across the prairie like they were going to charge into the mass of Apache, and some of the enemy saw them and started firing rifles in their direction. Henry hoped they were the mediocre marksmen that Stretch and Murphy had assured him they were. At about fifty yards from the warriors, Henry waved a halt, and in a few minutes time they were in line propped on one knee firing at the Indians. Gunfire was coming from the trench-like arroyo, leaving the Apache obviously confused as to where to focus.

Then the horse herd busted out from behind the butte in a cloud of dust heading southwest of the conflict. Chaos ensued. Some of the Apache broke off and chased after the horses. Several dropped to the ground wounded or dead. They were baffled, uncertain where to retreat. Finally, those who remained turned away from the fight and chased after their comrades who were pursuing the mounts. This battle was over.

Henry and his soldiers retrieved their mounts and led them toward the soldiers in the arroyo. One had already climbed out and was waving to them. He saw Stretch and Landry ride out from behind the butte, leading four saddled Army horses. Henry approached the ravine with apprehension. This had to be the missing patrol, and Jordy was not among them. The three soldiers he could see now were all colored.

As he walked up to a husky man with sergeant's stripes on his sleeve, the soldier saluted and spoke with a thunderous voice. "You are a welcome sight, Lieutenant. I figured we would all be buzzard food before the day was out if we was lucky enough not to be taken captive by them savages."

"I see you're from the Ninth Regiment. Was Lieutenant Dixon with you?"

"Yessir. He still is. We've got to get him out of this ditch and to a surgeon. He's hurt bad."

Without another word, Henry handed Valiant's reins to one of the privates and rushed to the arroyo, sliding down the slope to the floor not more than six feet below the rim. He landed not five feet from his friend who lay with his back resting against the slope, still holding his Army Colt in readiness for the final assault. He stared at Henry with furrowed brow.

He spoke with a choking, raspy voice. "Flip, where the hell did you come from?"

Henry moved to his friend's side, noting the blood-soaked left trouser leg. "You're wounded."

"That ain't tomato sauce on my pantleg, mister."

Henry dug a penknife from his pocket, and the razor-sharp blade quickly sliced the pantleg free from Jordy's leg. He was aghast at the torn, swollen flesh about the knee, crusty with dry blood and oozing pus.

Jordy said, "Bad as it feels?"

"It's not good. I assume there's a bullet lodged somewhere around your knee."

"Very astute."

"It hasn't been cleaned or bandaged."

"Nope. We were on the run. We hit two bunches. First ones just made off with half our horses after cutting our herd guard's throat during his watch. That put some of us afoot, so we took turns being infantry and started the long walk back to the encampment along the Rio Grande. Three days later, this band ambushed us. That must have been late afternoon two days ago now. I took the slug in the knee. Three men died when the Apache struck. Two wounded besides me. They since died. The others helped me and the other wounded to this ravine. The Apache waited us out yesterday, but I knew they wouldn't go another day before they finished the job. Just letting us get thirstier and tired out."

Henry turned back to the wound, remembering that Sergeant Murphy had some medical experience, and they had a full medical supply bag on the packhorse. "Jordy, you stay put. I'll get some help to haul you out of here. Sergeant Murphy's the next thing to a surgeon."

"Do you think I'm going to get up and walk out of here?"

As Henry climbed out of the ravine, he was reassured by the fact that Jordy had not lost his wry wit and tongue. When he was over the rim and back on his feet again, he surveyed the surrounding landscape. The Apache had disappeared, and he expected they were still chasing horses. He saw Stretch and Private Landry riding at little more than a walk coming their way leading four saddled Army horses. Murphy was talking to several of the formerly besieged soldiers, and he called to the sergeant. "Sergeant Murphy. Bring the medical bag and choose a few men to help you remove Lieutenant Dixon from the ravine. He's badly wounded. Knee."

It was nearly an hour past high noon when Murphy and Henry knelt by Jordy Dixon, who was conscious but semi-delirious. "What do you think, Sarge?" Henry asked.

"Ain't good. Been too long and some infection has set in. I wouldn't dare tamper with the slug. Imbedded in bone, I'm guessing. We've got to get him to one of the camp surgeons fast."

Henry hated to separate from Jordy, but he had a mission. "We'll need a litter to carry him on."

"I've got two men out finding wood for that. Trees are a bit scarce in this country, but they'll find something. We'll get the dead buried before we pull out—-that is if you want me to go with the party."

"You've become a mind reader, Sergeant. Yes, you're the only one with the medical know-how to tend to the patient, and an officer should lead the men back. I will continue the scouting mission with Private Hooper, and I want to take Corporal Mitchell with us as well. You will take what is left of the Tenth and our other three men with you."

"They aren't taking my leg. They'll have to kill me first."

Henry started at the sound of Jordy's voice. He had evidently returned to lucidity long enough to understand what was happening. "Jordy. Just listen to the surgeons. I'll talk to you as soon as I return. I'm hoping we won't be far behind you. We may even catch up."

Chapter 31
Jordy

OF COURSE, OLD Flip completed his mission. Stretch located Victorio by tracking the Apache that had attacked my patrol. It appears that they were congregating for a retreat to Mexico. Colonel Grierson ordered a massive sweep of cavalry from the north to drive the enemy across the Rio Grande. There were no deaths or wounded, however, because the Indians were long gone by the time soldiers arrived.

Word came to Fort Davis not long after our return that the Mexican army had confronted Victorio and his renegades and killed the famous war leader. Grierson got some credit for the accomplishment, but as was his nature, he shared it with Flip and Stretch. With Flip's support, Stretch was soon wearing his sergeant's stripes again. Darn it. I always wanted to become a hero without risk or scratch.

I escaped with my leg pretty much intact. The good Doctor Taryn Blair looked after me during a three-week stay in the post hospital after we returned to Fort Davis. The battlefield surgeons had removed the slug from my knee bone, but it was nip and tuck for that first week whether infection was going to claim the leg. I told Taryn that they would have to kill me before they amputated my leg, and she told me that was the stupidest thing she had ever heard. She offered to pull the trigger if I really meant it.

Things were cold between us most of the time I was confined to the hospital. She checked on me three or four times a day, and when I was feeling better, I suggested she might crawl under the blankets with me. She just glared at me, evidently having lost her sense of humor. I figured that maybe that was the beginning of the end for us.

Once again, Flip came to my rescue. It was several days before my hospital release, and he was sitting on the stool next to my hospital bed. He was the acting quartermaster for Fort Davis now and seemed to move easily into the job. Taryn reported on him daily, and it annoyed me a bit that she praised him so much. "The merchants in town love him," she said, "and the troops respect him. A few of the officers resent him, though."

"Sorry I haven't been by for three or four days," Henry said. "This quartermaster job has turned into a twenty-four-hour a day responsibility. Feels like it anyhow. Dr. Blair keeps me posted on your progress."

Now what did that mean? I did not like the idea that Flip was seeing Taryn so much. "Well, she keeps me posted on what you are doing, too. Sometimes I get the feeling God has taken over the quartermaster's job."

Henry chuckled. "Afraid not, but He can have it. I'm a field officer, not a bookkeeper. That's the nightmare, keeping track of the merchandise that's sold or distributed to the troops. And then the merchants in town sell and trade to the Army and we sell and trade back. I've got to account for every penny and compile written reports. This duty can't end soon enough. But I came to talk about you and Taryn."

"About me and Taryn?"

"Yes. She says you're going to take a medical discharge."

"Yep. I'll stay on through the winter. Maybe you can get me assigned to help you out at the commissary or something until March first. That's my release date. I could've left before, but I need some time to figure out what I do next. As you know, I don't mind the early out, but I'm going to have a knee that won't bend back right, and I'll be using a cane for a long time, maybe till I'm six feet under."

"Taryn . . . Doctor Blair's contract is up the first of April. She's not staying on here."

So they were first name users. Why was Flip trying to cover it? "You can use her first name. I know Doctor Blair's first name, and I daresay there aren't others with that handle at the fort."

"Just trying to be respectful, but, yes, I do count Taryn as a friend."

"Just don't get too friendly."

"Now, don't get your dander up. I'm here mostly to talk about you and Taryn."

"Well, she hadn't told me about her contract being up."

"She will soon enough. I'm here to yank you off your ass and tend to her."

"What in the hell are you talking about?"

"Ask her to marry you. She's in love with you, and you're in love with her. Now do something about it."

"Don't see how it's your concern. She wouldn't want a cripple anyhow."

"You sure won't find out if you don't ask. She's going to get away if you don't pull the line in."

"You really think she'd marry me?"

"I do. But what have you got to lose by asking her regardless?"

"My dignity."

"What dignity?" Henry stood. "I've got work to do. Maybe you should think about yours."

Not more than a half hour later, Taryn stopped by to look at the knee, which was healing quite well now. It occurred to me that she no longer needed to check that ugly knee three or four times a day. Maybe she wanted to see me.

She was leaning over my knee, her fingers gently probing the flesh about the healing wound, when I said, "Will you marry me, Taryn?"

She froze for an instant, then turned and looked at me, her turquoise-blue eyes incredulous. "What did you say?"

"One more time. I love you. Will you marry me, be my wife?"

Her brow furrowed, and she stared at me. "Are you serious?"

"I'm serious."

"It's not just because you're horny?"

I grinned. "Well, that too. But I'll still love you after I've had my way."

She stepped nearer and bent over and pressed her lips to mine with anything but a chaste kiss. I almost begged her to join me under the sheets but thought better of it. She pulled away. "Yes, Lieutenant Jordan Dixon, I will marry you."

I don't think I had ever been so happy in my life, and I had all I could do to keep from bawling like a baby. "I will leave it to you to work out the details."

"The day you leave the hospital. I'll talk to the post chaplain and arrange for the chapel. Henry, of course, will be best man. Annie Nolan will be my attendant and witness. You will move into my quarters until we leave here. Did I mention my contract is up early April?"

"We'll have to figure out where we go after that."

"Fort Sill. We'll talk about it later." She gave me a less passionate kiss and disappeared like a phantom. Was I just hallucinating about what just happened? And how in blazes had she made all these decisions so quickly? Were she and Henry engaged in a conspiracy?

I would never learn about a possible conspiracy to drag me to the alter, but why worry about how this all came about? Marriage to Taryn was what I dreamt about, so how can one complain about the fulfillment of his dreams, however it comes about? Taryn made the arrangements as she promised she would, and my only task was to hobble to the chapel. We did the deed with Henry at my side with a grin pasted on his face. I still wonder if Mollie Dwyer was on his mind that day. I know he loved that woman, and the presence of her sister Annie had to be a reminder of his parting with Mollie.

Anyhow, the knot got tied, and Taryn led me to her quarters, where I learned that Henry, under her supervision, had collected and delivered all my personal effects, most of which Taryn had already put away. My challenge would be to find the dang things. Taryn was granted three days off hospital duties, and we honeymooned in her quarters. Suffice it to say that my gimpy knee was not a hinderance, and, of course, all maneuvers were under a physician's supervision.

We did take a bit of time to discuss the future. Taryn informed me that Flip had arranged for my assignment to the post commissary, probably not a difficult task since nobody knew what to do with me pending discharge. I learned that she planned to establish her own clinic in the civilian areas adjacent to Fort Sill but had been assured contract work on the post would be available for whatever time she was willing to be on duty.

One afternoon when we lay in bed, I said, "So you are still going to be an Army surgeon at Sill?"

"When we first get there. But the area around Fort Sill will grow indefinitely, and there are the Comanche and Kiowa on the reservations. Once I establish a good private practice, I'll give up the Army work, but that may take several years. A private practice will give more flexibility for family."

"Family?"

"Children. You do know what causes babies, don't you? It appears we are going to have ample opportunity. I have considered the timing of our previous trysts. That will not be so easy now that we are sharing a bed every night. We'll just see what happens."

I was not certain what she meant. The woman kept my head spinning half the time, but I was not ready to talk about babies. "You seem to have your future all plotted out. What am I going to do at Fort Sill?"

"You said you wanted to write, sell books. I thought you might give that a try. There is a newspaper there that pays by the column inch. You could bring in a bit of income that way. I should make enough money to keep a roof over our heads and feed us. I have savings to help set up a clinic. Until the clinic is operating full-time, perhaps you could be in the office to schedule appointments and write in between. You will figure it out. You never give yourself enough credit. Well, I would never marry an idiot. I am not the least concerned that you will not be a success at whatever you choose to do."

"Well, I did like Fort Sill, and it is a busy place. If I'm sitting on my ass up there, it's because I've found a way to make money at the same time."

The future was looking pretty good for Taryn and me. I always tended to see the downside of things, but she had a way of lifting me up. I didn't know that day, though, that my concerns would soon turn to Flip.

Chapter 32
The Lost Funds

ENRY WAS COMING to appreciate the quartermaster's burden on a military post. Wagon loads of supplies arrived every other day. The Army exchanged some supplies with local merchants, sold some and bought some. Soldiers sometimes purchased items on credit with promises to pay for the merchandise on payday. It was the quartermaster's job to collect.

The quartermaster or his staff had to keep records of every transaction, submit reports to the post commandant's office weekly and explain anything that did not reconcile on the reports. Money was to be sent periodically to headquarters in San Antonio.

He struggled through the job during the winter and thought he was doing well enough, although he hoped to be relieved soon. Things changed with the arrival in early March of 1881 of Colonel William Rufus Shafter and his regimental staff to take command of Fort Davis. Henry learned quickly that the colonel did not like him much, for whatever reason, and that he had better keep his books in order.

The message was imparted just a few days after the new commandant's arrival. Henry was summoned to the colonel's office for an undisclosed purpose. He was only a bit apprehensive when he departed the quartermaster and commissary office north of the corrals and walked the twists and turns that took him to the north end of the parade ground where the post commander, his adjutant, and the sergeant major were provided offices.

This was the first time he had even seen Shafter, and when he was escorted into the office, he was surprised to see a bear-like, graying man who stood an inch or two short of six feet but would not weigh less than two hundred fifty pounds. He had shaggy eyebrows and a full mustache that could use a trim. The colonel was standing in front of the window when Henry stepped in, and he waited a bit before he turned and faced the quartermaster.

Henry saluted. "Lieutenant Flipper reporting as ordered, sir."

Shafter returned a casual salute and waved Henry to a chair in from his desk. He did not offer a handshake as some superior officers might have at the first meeting. Before he spoke, Shafter stared at Henry a few moments with his cold blue eyes peering out from the shelter of the thick eyebrows. He nodded toward the chair in front of his desk and then returned to his own chair. "Sit down, Lieutenant."

"Yessir." Henry sat down on the straight-back chair, facing the commanding officer.

The colonel said, "You are the quartermaster, I am informed. Important job. You've got to keep the post supplied. That means purchasing from local businessmen and the few ranchers we've got in these parts. Cattle, horses, flour, most of the food staples. More than one quartermaster has made himself wealthy by taking a commission from the sellers for awarding contracts for such merchandise. I trust that you have done no such thing."

Meaning, of course, that Shafter suspected him of taking such bribes. "No, sir, I have not."

"Well, regardless, I will be replacing you with my regimental quartermaster when he arrives, but that may be a month or two. I expect you to offer me complete ac-countings weekly until such time. You may be expected to continue commissary duties indefinitely. We will dis-cuss this at another time. Questions?"

"No, sir."

After Shafter's arrival, Henry's situation changed dramatically. The officers who arrived with the colonel seemed to avoid him, and several became friendly with Lieutenant Nordstrom, Mollie Dwyer's betrothed, and his own nemesis. His relationships with other officers had always been more strained at Fort Davis than at Fort Sill, where he had been generally accepted and formed friendships with other officers. The departure of Major McLaughlin and the present absence of Colonel Grierson gave birth to a hostile atmosphere in his mind.

He was relieved of quartermaster duties when his replacement arrived but remained in charge of the com-missary and learned quickly that the new quartermaster expected him to continue with most of his prior respon-sibilities, absent the title.

Other friendly officers had been transferred. Captain Nolan was still congenial, but Henry's detachment from Mollie had put an awkward distance between them. Jordy and his bride would be departing for Fort Sill in a month's time. As an officer, his social interaction with the colored enlisted men, who far outnumbered the white officers on the post, was limited. Besides, the commissary duties left little time for socializing.

He was uneasy with handling commissary funds, which had previously been tended to by a now transferred sergeant. Jordy assisted with the clerking there but because of his pending discharge bore no official responsibility. Colonel Shafter instructed Henry that safekeeping of the funds was his responsibility. There was no secure safe, so Henry commenced taking the funds to his quarters at night and storing them in a trunk that had travelled with him from his West Point days.

The arrangement in his quarters was complicated by the fact that a young woman, Lucy Smith, stored some of her clothing and personal items in the trunk. Lucy, a young, colored woman, was Henry's cook, laundress and housekeeper, who officially maintained her residence in a tent with another woman. She was a pretty, petite, sweet-dispositioned creature, however, and soon enough ended up in Henry's bed, where she spent many of her nights. The two lovers were friends but neither expected a future beyond Fort Davis.

Henry informed Colonel Shafter he was keeping commissary funds in his quarters and that he would move them to such other place as might be ordered, suggesting that acquisition of another safe might be helpful. Shafter told him to keep the funds in his quarters until he was relieved of responsibility, which should be a matter of days.

Henry complained to Jordy one morning at the commissary. "I don't like keeping the money in my quarters. Nordstrom knows because he asked me the other day if I was operating a bank out of my quarters, said he could use a loan. I can count on his having told others. I hope my replacement comes soon."

"What about the new quartermaster? Can't he take charge of the money?"

"He says he's not responsible for commissary funds and that it's my worry, but I'm responsible to him for my inventory and such. It doesn't make much sense."

Jordy said, "Does the Army ever make sense? I know you're dedicated, but I can't say I'm sorry to be moving on, but not quite as soon as I thought."

"Why not?"

"They can't find a replacement for Taryn here at Davis yet, and they've offered her a substantial bonus to stay on till October. We talked about it and agreed to extend the contract. The extra money will help her set up a practice near Fort Sill."

"But you will be discharged in a few weeks."

"That won't change, but I'm going to look for a job in town. I've got acquainted with a lot of the merchants working here, and those folks love you for some unexplainable reason. I thought you might put a word in for me if we invite you to dinner again next week."

"Two dinners. Jed Michels at the livery said he was desperate for somebody who can read and write and do numbers. He does a huge horse business, a lot of it with the Army. He needs a clerk for paperwork and keeping track of what he's paid for critters and what he sells them for. Inventory stuff like you help with here. I'll write up a general letter of recommendation but check with Jed first. He'll treat you right."

"I'm riding fine with the gimpy leg now, and we'll still have Taryn's quarters on the post. I'll just be a civilian spouse and ride into work every day. Hell, the business section of town runs up to the fort's edge. I could probably walk it. Taryn says that would be good for my leg."

Henry was glad Jordy would be around a spell yet. With the new commanding officer, it would be nice to have his friend nearby to listen to his grumbling. It did not appear he would be relieved of commissary duties anytime soon.

A few weeks later, Henry reconciled his commissary records and determined he should have $3,791.77 on hand

and sent notification to the Commissary General's office in Washington, D.C. of the amount. That night he counted his funds in his quarters and could only come up with slightly over two thousand dollars cash. His heart raced and he was struck with a sudden sense of panic.

He must account for the shortfall. He had a bank account in San Antonio and had no confirmation of a recent balance. He was anticipating royalty funds to be deposited there by the publisher of his West Point memoir, *The Colored Cadet at West Point*, for more than fifteen hundred dollars. He wrote a draft in the amount of $1,440.43 on the account payable to himself to cover the shortfall. He would endorse and place it with the other funds hoping that the publisher's funds would reach the bank before the draft completed its journey to San Antonio.

But where was the cash? Some could be accounted for by credit. Although soldiers were expected to pay cash for purchases, it was not unusual to extend credit till the next payday. These were treated as cash sales in his records and cash from the current period was sometimes used to cover the reporting amount. The same was done with some of the local business purchases, usually adjusted when merchandise was sold to the fort.

Still, something was not right, and he would likely need to absorb any actual loss personally. He had been foolish and sloppy in the management of funds. He had no excuses, but he would work his way through this dilemma to save his Army career. He endured a sleepless night that night and had no interest in making love to the woman who shared his bed.

Several days later, he appeared in Shafter's office with a report showing the correct amount of funds and advising the colonel that the funds had been sent to the commissary office in San Antonio. He was lying, buying time for funds from the publisher to be deposited in his bank.

"You are lying, Lieutenant," Shafter said. "I have a telegram from the commissary agent I received this morning informing me the money has not arrived. I don't like liars, Mister Flipper. You are confined to quarters and relieved of your duties at the commissary. Lieutenant Frank Edmunds will assume your responsibilities. My adjutant, First Lieutenant Louis Wilhelmi, will be placed in charge of investigating this matter. I trust you will cooperate with these gentlemen."

At first, he thought of suggesting that the funds simply had not arrived yet, but he would only buy a few days' time and then he would be found out. He had already sullied himself with a single falsehood, and he had always thought of himself as a truthteller. He would not compound his lies. He must continue searching for the facts.

The money or an explanation for the shortage was somewhere. He had not embezzled it. He was guilty of stupidity but not dishonesty.

When Henry returned to his quarters, he found Lucy preparing lunch. As they ate together at the small table, he explained his problem with the lost funds. He did not suspect her of taking the money and did not suggest it, but she was defensive.

"I did not touch the money, Henry. I would never do that. I ain't a thief."

"I know you wouldn't, Lucy. I just wanted to make you aware that you might be questioned."

"I don't think I should be here until this all clears up."

He was thinking the same thing but was glad he was not forced to suggest it. "I suppose it might be best."

"I will take care of the dishes and collect my things as soon as we finish eating."

They had not finished lunch before there was a sharp rapping on the door. He got up to respond. When he opened it, he was faced by Adjutant Wilhelmi and Lieutenant Edwards, his successor in the commissary.

Wilhelmi said, "We are here to search your quarters, Lieutenant, and to inform you that you should consider yourself under arrest." The men stepped into the kitchen-parlor of the two-room residence, and Wilhelmi saw

Lucy at the table. "Ma'am, it is best you leave. I will likely wish to speak with you later."

Lucy stood, "May I change first?"

"If you do it quickly."

Lucy disappeared into the bedroom, while the two visitors commenced rifling Henry's desk drawers. They recovered assorted coins which they counted and left on the desktop. Henry remained silent.

Next, they conducted a personal search, asking him to turn his pockets inside out. A few bills and coins fell to the floor, but Henry figured there would be no more than twenty dollars. When Lucy exited the bedroom, Wilhelmi said, "Lieutenant Flipper, you will accompany Lieutenant Edwards to the bedroom where he will continue the search. I will escort Miss Smith to Colonel Shafter's office. He wishes to speak with her."

Henry could not imagine why Shafter would wish to speak with Lucy, but there was nothing he could do about it. He was embarrassed by the bedroom search. His clothes were intermingled in the closet with Lucy's, and several pairs of her shoes were slid under the bed. It would have been clear to any observer that she was more than his maid. Edwards did find a few loose checks from commissary customers in the trunk, but they were worthless to anyone but the Army.

Henry felt the search of his quarters was unnecessarily invasive with Edwards rifling through his underwear, and Lucy's, holding up each item and lifting his eyebrows. The search had just been completed when Wilhelmi returned nearly two hours after his departure.

He found himself speechless, however, when Wilhelmi walked into the room with two envelopes in his hand and said, "Your friend Lucy Smith surrendered these two envelopes stuffed with checks that she had hidden in the bosom of her blouse and apparently planned to take with her. Can you explain?"

"No, sir, I cannot." And he could not. He knew nothing about more checks. And they would be worthless in private hands. Pieces of paper. Where was this going?

Chapter 33
The Prisoner

ENRY STAYED IN his quarters, technically under arrest. A guard was even stationed outside his quarters. This was unusual because officers arrested for offenses other than treason or acts of violence were generally confined according to the honor system. To flee would be the equivalent of desertion which could invite a firing squad.

Alone, he brooded about his dilemma, gripped by depression he had never experienced. And there was anger. What was Lucy doing with the checks? They were unendorsed and represented funds received beyond the period of the shortfall, so they did not cover the deficiency. He refused to see her as a thief, but her action had worsened his situation, although he supposed it put him in a position to blame her for the shortfall which he still saw as his responsibility.

He was not allowed visitors, and meals far below Lucy's standards were delivered to his quarters. He missed that young woman more than he ever imagined he would. They had in many respects become like husband and wife, and it had been rather nice to have a sense of home and family. He assumed that was over now. His only concerns were clearing his name and retaining his position in the Army.

After four days, a most welcome visitor was admitted to his quarters: former Second Lieutenant Jordan Dixon. There were three raps on the door, an old West Point signal the two shared, and Jordy stepped in. Attired in denims and a faded blue cotton shirt, it seemed strange to see his friend out of uniform.

They shared a firm handshake, and Henry stepped back to look at his friend. "How in blazes did you get in here?"

"I got a note from Shafter that says I got a half hour to check on your wellbeing. Taryn went to the colonel himself and threatened to write a letter to his superiors if she was not able confirm that you were not being mistreated. I am her emissary. I learned you were under arrest early on. Word travels fast around an Army post. I just didn't know how to get to you."

"I'm glad you married above yourself."

"Well, I won't deny it, but time's wasting. Tell me what I can do."

"I've got a list. Come in here."

"I should have known you would have a list."

"Come over to the table, and we'll sit down and go over it."

Jordy's eyes ran over the two-page list. "A lawyer's at the top. Will they allow a civilian to represent you?"

"I don't know, but it can't hurt to have someone outside the military sending advice my way. My chances of getting a schooled lawyer aren't great in the Army. I'm hoping no charges are filed, but if they are, some officer will probably be appointed to defend me. On the list you will find books on military law. I need to be prepared to defend myself."

"The list says 'sell horses.' Why? Surely you wouldn't sell your stallion Valiant?"

"I'm going to need money to pay back the shortfall. I can't explain how it happened. My own bad judgment, outright stupidity maybe."

"I've known you too long to buy that. I'll talk to Taryn. We have money saved back. I know she would agree to a loan."

"You've got plans. I can't let you risk those."

"The horses would be security for some of the loans. Just slow down and give this some thought. You were always warning me to stop and think about things before I acted. Well, now it's your turn. I'll find out what's going on and get word to you some way till you're freer to talk. Taryn and I are with you wherever this goes."

They continued talking until a loud knock on the door signaled their time had expired. Jordy's last words before he went out the door were, "Flip, I've always told folks that you are the toughest old horse I ever saw and that you cannot be broken. Whatever happens, don't make a liar out of me."

He was close to broken before Jordy said that. Henry would always remember those words, but they came especially to mind several days later when Wilhelmi visited, accompanied by a rifle-bearing soldier, a colored man from the Ninth Regiment according to his insignia. The adjutant had a smug look on his face when he announced, "Lieutenant Flipper, I am here to inform you that you have been charged with embezzlement of government funds and conduct unbecoming of an officer and a gentleman. You will immediately be escorted by Private Cooper to the guardhouse."

Henry was stunned, but he knew that Wilhelmi would enjoy an opportunity to respond to any protests and would be quick to have the guard rough him up a bit. He picked up his hat and accompanied Cooper on the walk to the guardhouse. Wilhelmi headed for the commandant's office, obviously to inform Shafter that the prisoner had been moved to the guardhouse.

In less than ten minutes Henry was incarcerated in a stone cell 6.5 feet long and 4.5 feet wide. The door was shut and locked. He could see outside and collect a bit of air through a three-inch window slit in the wall, which also provided his only light. He could make out muffled voices from the corridor outside where other prisoners were housed. He guessed their offenses were less serious, brawling, drunkenness and the like.

He was sickened over the turn of events. He was well aware of the consequences of being charged with "conduct unbecoming of an officer and a gentleman." It was stated in an Article of War that any officer convicted of such a charge "shall be dismissed from the service." His career was at stake. Such was his despair that for the first time in his life, suicide crossed his mind. But Jordy had said he could not be broken.

Chapter 34
Jordy

WITHIN A FEW hours after Henry Flipper was escorted to the guardhouse, a young, colored orderly who assisted my wife at the hospital rode into the livery with a message from Taryn. She waited while I read the short note. "Henry formally charged. Placed in guardhouse. We must talk."

I said, "Tell Doctor Blair that I will be there as soon as possible." I immediately went to the horse lots behind the livery that stretched for some fifty acres beyond. We cared for nearly a hundred critters there and that meant moving a lot of hay, because that barren acreage would barely support two. I was confident that my boss, Jed Michels, would tell me to go back to the fort. He thought the world of Flip and had been one of the leaders in collecting donations from businessmen to cover Flip's money shortfall.

I found him with two of the other hands loading a hay wagon. Jed preferred the sweat work and left the book-work to me, which suited me just fine since I was not looking for a career as a livestock man. I had enough of that growing up.

I told Jed, a short, stocky man with what is now called a handlebar mustache, about the message I received from Taryn. "She seems to think I am needed at the post to help Henry," I said.

"Then you'd better get your ass out there." He put his pitchfork down. "But I got something to send with you. It's in the safe."

I followed him to the warped, plank-walled office where I worked at a marred, shaky desk. He bent over to open the safe that no longer required a combination and pulled out a big envelope. "Over two thousand dol-lars cash money in here donated by business folks in the town. The wife's got a list of who gave and how much. That's to go to Henry's debt. You tell him that the Fort Davis town folks are behind him."

"I will do that, and I thank you. If we need a bit more, I know where I can get it." Taryn and I had already agreed we would advance whatever funds we could to help Henry out. That was another reason I loved that woman so. She is more careful with money than I tend to be, but she's generous with a friend. She always understood my loyalty to Henry and accepted it. If she had not caught me first, I'm betting she would have tossed her baited hook at old Flip and pulled him in. I was a little worried when they first met that she might throw me back, but I got lucky, and she kept me.

I went promptly to the Army hospital but had to wait until Taryn finished amputation of a gangrenous toe of all things. Most of her work does not seem all that glamorous, but she loves it and contributed more to the household than I did during those early times—never once pointed that out to me, though.

When I finally met her in that closet they called an office, she brought me up to date on Flip. "They've got him penned up in one of those cages they call a cell. That's not standard procedure for an officer facing a court martial."

I may not have mentioned that Taryn and two brothers were raised on Army posts, and that General Carlton Blair was her father. He was then an undersecretary of state or some such thing. I suppose I'll meet the old rascal someday. Her mother died when Taryn was in high school, and she ended up at a boarding school back east. At that time, her brothers were already at West Point. I suppose that explains her desire not to stray too far from the Army.

"What is standard procedure?" I asked.

"They are confined to their residence. It makes sense. Why would any man with a brain in his head run and risk desertion charges. I have telegraphed Daddy asking him to investigate the Henry Flipper case."

I told her about the money and then confessed. "Before I rode back to the fort, I stopped at the *Fort Davis Republican* in town. I told the editor, George Carpenter, about Henry's dilemma and offered to write an inside story."

"You are trying to cash in on this?"

"I will get fifty cents per column inch. If it is any good, he will try to farm the story out to some big city papers. I will get half of any royalties from that. I'm on my way to being a professional writer."

"It's about time. We bought that new Remington typewriter, and I've never heard a click or a clack from it other than when you are studying those typing instructions and trying to learn the keyboard."

"It's not easy, but I've got incentive. Maybe we can help Henry if his story gets told."

I delivered the money directly to Colonel Shafter's office and insisted upon seeing him. When I was admitted to his office, I marched up to his desk and did not sit down. It was such a good feeling not to salute anymore. I placed the envelope, which now included my draft for over two hundred dollars. "Henry Flipper's shortfall contributed by civilian businesspeople. Nobody believes that Henry would embezzle a nickel."

Shafter glared at me. "Is that your business for the day?"

"One other thing. I can assure you that the eyes of the nation will be on Fort Davis regarding the administration of the case."

Shafter chuckled. "I think that is highly unlikely, Mister Dixon."

Well, Shafter was wrong about that much. In a matter of two days, Henry's case was winning national headlines, not all positive, and yours truly was earning a byline and royalties. The Republican editor hired me to write updates on the story at twice the initial rate and agreed to continue to market my production to the national press for a royalty split. At this stage of my budding career, I had no notion of how to cut out the middleman. That knowledge would come later.

It took nearly a week more, but soon Taryn received a telegram from her father: "The Lieutenant will be released from confinement. Contact Herbert if legal assistance required. And I want to meet your husband, the famous writer."

I was at my typewriter when Taryn brought the telegram home that evening and placed it in front of me. "Don't let your head get too big," she said.

I tried to be modest. "Your father was just joshing. Who's Herbert?"

"My brother, Mister Famous Writer. Herbie. I've mentioned him hundreds of times. Major Herbert Blair."

"He's a lawyer?"

"No, but Daddy must think he knows someone."

I was still spending mornings at the livery but devoted my afternoons to reporting. Jed didn't mind. He saved salary expenses, and I still got my work done. "Flip gave me the list of things to work on. I spoke with J.M. Dean, the leading town attorney, and he was willing to help, but Shafter and Wilhelmi made it clear that a civilian lawyer would not be allowed to represent Flip in a court martial proceeding."

"Didn't he help Lucy Smith?"

"Yes, but she was jailed in town at the request of Shafter. They held her for a week before the prosecutor decided there was no evidence sufficient to prosecute her for theft of any kind. The checks in the envelopes that were taken from her were payable to the Commissary.

They were not endorsed, and she could have done nothing with them. The only possible witness is Flip, and neither Lawyer Dean nor the town prosecutor was allowed to speak with him. He wouldn't have helped them anyway."

"Even if her guilt would help absolve him."

"No. I'm sure he was not in love with her, but he cared about her, and I have no doubt they were intimate. It would be contrary to Flip's nature to turn on a woman who had meant something to him. Sometimes we are blind about the wrongs of those we care about, too."

"You don't let me get by with much."

"I'll throw those words back at you."

There was a soft rapping at the door. I got up. "I'll get it." I went to the door and opened it, surprised to see a sober-faced Sergeant Milo Murphy standing there. "Sergeant Murphy, good to see you. Won't you come in?" I stepped back, but Murphy remained planted.

He handed me an envelope and spoke in his distinctive gruff voice. "I did not give you this, but I will vouch for the man who gave it to me. Do what you will with it." He wheeled and walked briskly away.

Taryn came up behind me. "What was that all about? That was Sergeant Murphy."

"Let's find out." I opened the envelope and plucked out a single sheet of paper. Two items were handwritten and dated today, obviously copied from original telegraph wires. I read them aloud. "Henry Flipper's confinement to the guardhouse, though within the province of the Post Commander, is not usual, unless there be reasons to apprehend an escape. General William Tecumseh Sherman."

Taryn said, "And there is another."

"Yes." I continued. "This is from General Christopher Auger. It says, 'Both the Secretary of War and General of the Army require that this officer must have the same treatment as though he were white.' My friend Henry Flipper will be back in his quarters tomorrow morning if he has not already been moved there." I sighed. "I think your father interceded."

"Perhaps. But I sleep with a certain writer who probably had a greater impact." She smiled and gave me an embrace and kiss that made me forget all about Henry's problems.

"Uh, should we put some supper together?" I asked.

"Later." She took my hand and led me to heaven.

Chapter 35
The Lawyer

THE COURT MARTIAL convened at Fort Davis mid-September. The case would be heard by eleven officers, some of whom were summoned from other posts, by Brigadier General Auger of San Antonio, who signed the order appointing the court, although the adjutant general for the Department of Texas made the actual selection. The judge advocate, who would present the Army's case, was Captain John W. Clous of the 24th Infantry, a lawyer with considerable experience in such proceedings.

The judge advocate's role was to present the case impartially, but Henry learned quickly that Clous was essentially the prosecutor. It would be suicide for the defendant not to have his own legal counsel. He dispensed with any notion that he might represent himself and asked for more time to procure an attorney. The request was granted, and the court martial was rescheduled to commence on November 1. Jordy, who had been denied admission to the court, was waiting outside and walked with him to his quarters. Thankfully, an escort was no longer required.

When they reached Henry's quarters, Jordy brewed coffee on the coal cookstove and then placed two full cups on the table, and the men sat down to talk. Henry told Jordy about the delay in the hearing.

Jordy said, "Taryn has contacted her brother about a lawyer. He's on temporary assignment at Fort Sill. She expects to hear from him any day now."

"Nobody wants to touch this case, and I just can't pay for a civilian lawyer even though I've been granted permission to employ one. They start at a thousand dollars or more. And don't say that you and Taryn will help. You've done enough."

"But you have given me a new career. I feel guilty about that sometimes."

"Why? You have taken my story to the newspapers." He rolled his eyes. "Although a bit too objectively at times. You can write, Jordy, with words that common folks understand. Why did you hide that talent from me all these years?" He sensed he was making his friend uneasy and switched back to the lawyer issue. "Anyhow, I'm hoping Taryn's brother can help us. If he is at Sill, you should have a chance to meet him when you move next month."

"I won't be moving till the trial's over. Taryn's committed to go on duty the same day the trial starts. She will need to leave by the second week in October to make all the connections to get there. The stage road to San Antonio goes past Davis, so she will take that to San Antonio and use mostly rail connections from there. It's complicated, but she's got it figured out, of course."

"If you can't attend the trial, there's no point in staying here. How can you write about it?"

"Maybe your lawyer can get me in. If not, I have sources of information, including the defendant. And there is the matter of backing a friend. There's nothing more to talk about on that subject. I've already rented a room at a boarding house in town."

Jordy returned two days later with welcome news. "You should receive a letter soon from an officer who will volunteer his services as your attorney. Taryn's brother wrote to a lawyer he met at Fort McKavett, Texas. His name is Captain Merritt Barber. He is well educated with a bachelor's degree from Williams College in Massachusetts and a law degree from Ohio State Law College. He was a brevet brigadier general during the War of the Rebellion. You will have no cost, of course, since no officer defending another officer is permitted to charge for his services."

"If he is willing to defend me, I have no choice. I have heard it said that a person who defends himself has a fool for a lawyer. He is still at McKavett?"

"That's my understanding. It is only about two hundred miles from here. If you accept his services, he should have no problem getting here well in advance of the trial."

"That would be wonderful. It would give me an opportunity to tell him my side of the case."

Four days later, Henry received a letter via stagecoach from Captain Merritt Barber. The letter was very brief and recited that Barber had been following newspaper accounts of his pending court martial and that he would be honored to offer his services as legal counsel. If Henry wished to accept, he must send a formal request to Barber's commanding officer whose name and address was provided. Enclosed with the letter was a summary of Barber's civilian and military background. He could not imagine finding anyone more qualified. He promptly wrote the request to the commanding officer and another to Barber expressing his appreciation.

Captain Merritt Barber arrived by stagecoach two weeks before commencement of the trial and was escorted to Henry's quarters. Barber appeared to be a man in his early forties, younger than Henry had anticipated. He was of average height with brownish hair and a thick mustache. His attention was immediately drawn to the man's gentle, light-brown eyes that were obviously appraising his new client.

Henry extended his hand and received a firm grip from the lawyer. "I'm Henry Flipper, sir. Thank you for coming. Step into my quarters." The escort was carrying several bags in addition to the stuffed carpetbag in Barber's hand. "You may leave the bags in my quarters, Private Jones, until we make more permanent arrangements for the captain."

When the escort was dismissed, Barber said, "If it is all the same to you, Lieutenant, I would prefer to share your quarters while I am here. It will be convenient for conferring about strategies during the court martial and assure that you are not bothered by unwelcome guests."

"Whatever you wish, sir. You may have my room. Someone will check on my presence here in another hour, and I will request a cot and mattress for the parlor."

"I would not be comfortable removing you from your bed."

"And I would be very uncomfortable having a guest sleep in the parlor, especially a higher-ranking officer, sir. It will be no problem. You may wish to take your meals at officers' mess. The standards for prisoners are quite low."

'I will take my meals with you, and I assure you that the standards will improve." He made the statement softly but confidently.

"Well, sir, I usually have coffee midafternoon, and a friend of mine left cookies this morning. Would you care to join me?"

"An excellent idea. And henceforth in your quarters, there will be no 'sirs,' and we shall address each other as Henry and Merritt. Do you have any objection to that?"

"Not at all, sir . . . I mean Merritt."

Over coffee, the men discussed the case, Henry telling the lawyer about the events leading up to the charges. "I was careless. I used poor judgment. I am very embarrassed about all this, but I am not a thief. I want to remain in the Army and prove my worth."

Barber said, "I will be blunt. This case has received national attention because you are a colored man. You gained modest fame with your graduation from West Point. You are more famous—or perhaps I should say infamous—as a result of the charges you are facing. Do you believe your race has had anything to do with the charges?"

"No. I am responsible for my own mistakes. I am neither blind nor deaf, and I know there are those who are wary or do not like me because I am colored. I suspect Colonel Shafter carries a certain bias, and it probably goes beyond that with several others. I have occasionally wondered if there was a conspiracy among some to create this dilemma, but those are not rational thoughts. Even if this were so, and someone plotted a theft, it was my duty to protect the funds, and I should have taken steps to protect them."

"You seem to be reluctant to blame racial bias."

"The Army, on balance, has treated me well, and I have had more officers who were blind to my color than those who were not. All folks of whatever color deal with prejudice of one sort or another. I will not carry my color as an excuse."

"Commendable, I'm sure, but there is prejudice, and I intend to investigate its role here. Think about this and write down the names of those men who may have a grudge or not like you for any reason."

"I can do that much. A few have not been shy about communicating their dislike."

"I cannot help you if you do not communicate the full truth to me. Our conversations are confidential, and I hope you will come to trust me and tell me the whole story. Something is missing."

"Do you think I am lying to you?"

"Not directly. Let us call it errors of omission."

"I don't understand."

"Lucy Smith. You have not told me everything about Lucy Smith, and I am sensing that she is a bigger part of this case than anyone suspects—or wants to suspect."

"Our relationship went beyond her looking after my quarters and preparing meals. She often spent the night. There is nothing else to say."

"You truly do not think she could have taken the money?"

Henry shrugged but did not reply.

Barber said, "We will be talking more about Lucy. There is one thing I do want to caution you about."

"Yes."

"Your letter writing. You have written many letters to people about your situation, and some have chosen to make those public. One of those was to John Quarles, a New York lawyer you attempted to hire."

"Yes. Quarles is well known, and he is a colored man, who also was my teacher as a small child while he was still a slave. I hoped he might have some interest in my case, but he asked for more money than I could raise in ten years."

"And he gave your letter to New York newspapers for publication, a gross violation of ethical standards. No more letters to lawyers, newspapers or public officials. Family only."

"I understand."

"Are there Army officers or friends who might act as character witnesses, sign statements that you have been a competent officer, that sort of thing?"

"I like to think so."

"Work on that list also. Write me a summary of what you would expect them to say. Just a few sentences. I'm trying to keep your pen and pencil busy on constructive things." Barber smiled. "I like you, Henry. I cannot promise how this will turn out, but I will give you my best effort."

Henry was satisfied that he had the right lawyer.

Chapter 36
Jordy

I MET HENRY'S LAWYER a few days after Taryn left for Fort Sill. I would be moving to the boarding house the next day, so I did not have pristine quarters for hosting him. I had not seen Henry for a spell because we had been busy packing Taryn's things for her journey, and I knew Captain Barber was sharing Henry's residence now.

I liked the man instantly, and his calm demeanor exuded confidence. We sat on chairs in the parlor nursing afternoon coffees as we chatted. I apologized for being unable to offer anything more, and he just chuckled and remarked that he could not ever brew his own coffee when his wife was absent.

Barber said, "Henry tells me you are his best friend. I gather he is cautious about getting too close to people."

"I'd say that is true enough."

"I've read a lot of your articles about Henry's case. You have built quite a reputation for yourself."

"I don't know if that's good or bad."

"Very good, I assure you. I enjoy reading your work because while you always disclose your friendship, the stories are remarkably objective. You stick to the facts and never interject opinion unless it is identified as such."

"I would like to report on the trial, but I guess press admissions are very limited."

"Yes, the military has that prerogative, but the record will become available at some point."

"I'm thinking there might be a book here."

Barber nodded thoughtfully. "If I obtained permission for you to watch and take notes during the proceedings, I trust that you would continue your objective reporting?"

I did not hesitate. "I would certainly try. If bias creeps in it would not likely be favorable to the prosecution. I have an agent back east who will market the stories. I understand, however, that the Charles Guiteau trial in Washington will be competing for newspaper space at roughly the same time. It will likely draw more public attention." Guiteau was charged with the assassination of James A. Garfield.

Thus, I was present when the trial convened in the post chapel on November 1 with Colonel Galusha Pennypacker, a medal of honor recipient, presiding. Pennypacker was commander of the 16th infantry and enjoyed some fame as the youngest brevet major general in the Union Army during the Civil War, having enlisted at age sixteen and been promoted to the rank when he was just short of twenty-one years of age. At the time of the court martial, he would have been in his late thirties. A captain from the 16th also served on the court.

All officers sitting on the court, of course, were white, but there were no other colored officers serving in the Army. Interestingly, none of the officers were West Point graduates. What concerned Barber most was that, after the withdrawal of one court member, three officers from Shafter's Infantry remained on the ten-member court. Since Barber was from Pennypacker's 16th Infantry Regiment, however, it was difficult for him to object.

Several days were spent arguing preliminary matters, and I confess I nodded off more than once. The trial finally commenced following opening statements by Judge Advocate John Clous, a black-bearded imposing figure, and Henry's counsel, Captain Merritt Barber. The first witness called by Clous was Colonel Shafter who appeared extremely nervous. He gave three days of testimony, much of it about verification of the shortfall.

The hearing room became very tense when he testified about the search of Lucy Smith at his office. He admitted that in the presence of an orderly he had felt Lucy's torso and discovered the envelopes containing checks. Upon further questioning he explained that he had summoned his house servant to conduct a full search.

Barber pressed him about the search, "Did you direct your servant to strip Lucy?"

"I directed her to make a thorough search."

"Do you swear that you did not order her to be stripped naked?"

Shafter said, "I did not order her to be stripped, but I did tell the woman to examine every part of her clothing and see that there was nothing under them."

"Do you know if that was done?"

"I know that the woman told me it was done."

He testified he was not present in the office during the search but conceded that the search could have been witnessed by others through the office window. I wondered if a white woman would have been searched in such a manner.

Barber tried to make an issue of Henry's treatment as a prisoner, which probably was not relevant to the precise charges, but I suppose could have been evidence of biased treatment. After questioning Shafter about the reasons for Henry's unorthodox imprisonment pending the court martial, however, Clous objected to the line of questioning. Barber made a statement to the court that might open the bias issue. He said:

> I want to ask him this question for the purpose of showing that even the private soldiers of this command would not obey the orders which he had given in regard to confining an officer in the guardhouse. Even the private soldiers felt ashamed at the treatment being visited upon my client. Propositions were made to the accused to take him out of the guardhouse by force. He declined it. I wish to ask this witness if any such information came to his knowledge, then on the part of the defense we can show it.

Clous objected, of course, and Colonel Pennypacker cleared the hearing room, so the court could consider the objection privately. When the court reconvened, Pennypacker announced that Clous's objection was sustained. Henry never mentioned this publicly and like so many things, never would, and I never pressed him on it. If I asked him a question, and he remained silent, I always accepted silence as his answer.

The trial moved forward quickly after Shafter's testimony was completed. Wilhelmi and Edwards, the earlier searchers of Flipper's quarters and the commissary offices, each had a day or two of testimony supporting their findings. It seemed well rehearsed to me, but it brought nothing new to the case. Mostly, they talked about the receipts and coins they had stumbled across but nothing that linked any findings to the embezzlement charge. At worst, it seemed to me that Henry might be guilty of gross untidiness.

After the judge advocate rested his case, Barber presented the case for the defense. Several Fort Davis civilian merchants testified, attesting to Henry Flipper's integrity in his dealings with them and confirmed that they had made contributions to the fund to cover the shortfall.

The headline testimony was anticipated to be Lucy Smith's, but Barber had spoken with her and feared she would not be helpful. Mostly, Lucy "did not remember" anything. She confirmed that she cooked, washed, ironed, and cleaned the quarters for Henry, and she did not challenge when both attorneys referred to her living with him, although she never outright admitted the fact.

She did testify that she kept some of her belongings in a trunk that included commissary money but that the trunk was locked, and she had to ask Henry for keys. Although she said she could not even remember anything about the day of the search and Henry's arrest, she did testify that she had asked him for trunk keys to get some of her clothing when the officers were there.

Barber asked her, "Did you take out any papers and envelopes?"

"I had taken out two envelopes and put them in my bosom."

"What was the cause of your taking out the envelopes?"

"Because I was in this trunk, and I had taken some things out, and because I had a woman in there working that was not very honest."

Lucy testified that Henry had instructed her to keep the trunk locked and to return the keys whenever she left. She also said that she had taken the envelopes without Henry's knowledge. She could not remember if she had locked the trunk that day but thought she left the keys on the table.

Her memory lapses got worse after that. Barber asked, "Did you see Colonel Shafter that morning?"

"I don't remember whether I seen him or not. I was so scared."

"Did you go to Colonel Shafter's office?"

"I don't remember whether I went over there or not. I was scared to death."

"Where did you go during that day?"

"I went to jail for one place."

"Where were you when you were taken to jail? Where did you go from?"

"I don't know, Captain, because I was so scared. I don't know where I was taken from."

"What scared you?"

"I can't tell you. I don't know what scared me. I was scared, though."

She could not remember what happened to the envelopes she took from the trunk. She could remember little about Shafter except that she was frightened of him. Barber gave up, and was clearly upset by her lacking recall.

On cross-examination by Clous, she denied spending any nights in Henry's quarters, although substantial evidence pointed to the contrary. Clous elicited more "I do not remembers" and he also appeared frustrated. On balance she remembered nothing that either helped or hurt Henry's case.

The remainder of the defense was a parade of character witnesses, including more local merchants and Major N.B. McLaughlin, who gave Henry's performance as an officer a glowing endorsement. Barber was permitted to read a letter of commendation from Colonel Grierson, which the court allowed as a testimonial to Henry Flipper's character rather than as evidence.

The court adjourned until December 6.

Chapter 37
Flipper's Statement

CAPTAIN BARBER AND Flipper discussed at length the pros and cons of the defendant testifying under oath. Henry wanted to tell his story. He had not embezzled. He was guilty of stupidity in not securing the funds more carefully. He refused to believe that Lucy Smith would have taken the funds, although he conceded that her stories were inconsistent and confusing. Regardless, he had no proof of guilt on her part. She had been good to him, and he would make no accusation in the absence of conclusive evidence.

He could not shake his suspicion that Wilhelmi and Edmunds, possibly with his longtime rival Nordstrom's assistance, had somehow set him up for the embezzlement charge. Only a hallway separated his and Nordstrom's quarters. Could one or more of the officers have enticed Lucy's cooperation? It did not matter. He had no evidence, only his distrust of the men.

After an exchange that took place over several hours, Barber said, "Henry. You should not testify. That would give Clous the right to cross-examine. You are unable to explain what happened, and he will tear you to shreds. I do not think there is sufficient evidence to convict you on the embezzlement count. I am reasonably confident that will keep you out of prison."

"But the 'conduct unbecoming of an officer and a gentleman.' You are not so confident?"

"I must be honest with you. No. That is arbitrary and subjective. Beyond that, the punishment is uncertain. It could be a mere notation on your record or a severe reprimand with suspension of pay for a short period. Worst case: dismissal and discharge from the Army."

Henry found himself shaking and light-headed. "It is the dismissal that concerns me most."

"I can guarantee nothing."

"But is there a way I can speak directly to the court?"

"Yes. I think that the court would allow you to make a non-evidentiary statement, much like Colonel Grierson's. It would be considered by the court more on the issue of punishment and not on the matter of guilt or innocence. Clous would not be allowed to cross-examine."

Henry sighed. "I will prepare a statement for your review."

The day the court martial reconvened, the trial moved into its second month. Strangely, he felt more at ease today. He suspected it was because he was finally going to be allowed to speak in his own defense. He had written out his statement and would have the few pages in front of him on the lectern facing the court members, although he had retained the words substantially in his memory.

When General Pennypacker called upon him, he rose from the table he shared with his counsel and stepped to the lectern, his eyes briefly meeting those of the men who sat at the tables in front of him before he spoke, "I declare to you in the most solemn and impressive manner possible that I am perfectly innocent in every manner, shape or form, that I have never myself nor by another appropriated, converted or applied to my own use a single dollar or a single penny of the government . . ."

He explained that the money was kept in his quarters for security purposes because he was responsible for the funds and determined that was the safest course. He insisted that he had no idea where the money went or who took it. He reviewed his efforts to resolve the problem and admitted that the check he had written to cover the shortfall was not covered by bank funds. He insisted, however, that he honestly had expected a deposit from his publisher, Homer Lee & Co., to arrive in time to provide adequate funds, admitting that the firm still had not paid.

He emphasized again as he neared the end of his presentation that he had no knowledge regarding the disappearance of the funds, declaring, "I have no privity or knowledge and am not responsible except to make the amount good, and that I have done."

When Henry concluded his statement, Captain Barber made his own closing statement and pointed out to the court that the accused was not required to prove that he did not embezzle the money, but that it was for the government to prove that he did embezzle it and knowingly and willfully misappropriated the funds and applied them to his own use and benefit.

Barber said, "Have they done so? Where, when and by what testimony? There is not a syllable of proof of it."

The attorney pointed out the various achievements by Flipper during his life, observing that he had defied odds that only a colored man could appreciate. He suggested that Flipper's position as an Army officer was an anomaly and that the court's decision might determine the future for colored men as officers.

He concluded, "The question is before you whether it is possible for a colored man to secure and hold a position as an officer in the Army."

Chapter 38
Jordy

BARBER'S CLOSING ARGUMENT was effective and confirmed that Henry could not have procured better representation, but I had no confidence in how this would all turn out. Clous's closing statement was a rehash of the testimony, and thereafter the court went into closed session for several hours.

When the court reconvened, the verdict was read and Henry was found "Not Guilty" on Charge I, meaning he was acquitted of embezzlement. Regarding Charge II, he was found guilty on all counts. Thus, he was guilty of conduct unbecoming of an officer and a gentleman.

The shock to me came in the announced sentence. "And the court does therefore sentence him, Second Lieutenant Henry O. Flipper of the Tenth Regiment U.S.

Cavalry to be dismissed from the service of the United States."

Henry sat stone-faced in his chair, but I knew his pain had to be acute. I joined Henry and a despondent Captain Barber on the walk to Henry's quarters. When we arrived, I offered to leave if Barber wished to speak to his client in confidence.

Henry said, "No, Jordy, I want you here."

I volunteered to brew coffee and left Henry and the lawyer to talk privately for a bit. When I returned with cups and a coffee pot, Barber was explaining that a lengthy review of the process would take place. First review would be by General Augur as commander of the department of Texas. Judge Advocate General David Swain with Bureau of Military Justice in Washington would be next. He would make recommendations to President Arthur, who would make the final decision.

"The matter is out of our hands," Barber said. "No further evidence can be admitted. You can only wait, and it may be months. During that time, you remain an officer, technically under arrest."

"We have no control over how fast the process moves?"

"None." He hesitated. "Henry, I don't want to give you false hope, but General Augur or the president do have authority to change the verdict."

"For better or for worse?"

"In all honesty, either, but I cannot imagine it being worse. I would not anticipate a 'not guilty' ruling on the second count, but there could be a mitigation of the penalty. I had expectations it would not provide for outright dismissal from the Army."

"I guess I can hope for the best."

I could see from the downcast look on his face that Henry held little hope for a favorable outcome. The court martial had worn him down, and he was as near to whipped as I had ever seen him. From the way he was being treated, I could not imagine why he even wanted to stay in he Army, but I could never read Flip's mind. If I could, I would search his head till I found out what really happened. He might not have the whole story there, but he knew more than he ever told us.

Henry turned to me. "Jordy, it's time for you to head for Fort Sill. Taryn has been very patient, but she deserves to have her husband with her."

He was right, and we needed to get on with sinking roots there. Mail moved faster from Fort Sill now and rail was moving nearer and changing the world. It was important that I talk to Taryn and make decisions about just how I was going to make a living. It was clear to me already that income could not be counted upon in the writing business. "Yeah, I should make some arrangements, get rid of the last of our furnishings and that sort of thing. We'll have a good talk before I leave. I'll check with you when I have it all figured out."

I downed what was left in my coffee mug and headed into town. I had walked the short distance to the fort. It was late afternoon, and the sun was shining brightly, but somehow it seemed a lot colder than when I made the journey to the trial that morning. So much had happened, and now I was fighting a pounding headache.

I sent a telegram to Taryn the next morning informing her of the court martial's outcome and that I would be joining her at Fort Sill as soon as I figured out the route. She responded with a precise list of the connections I should make by coach and rail. She ended the message with the words. "Big news. Hurry. I still love you."

Now why did she have to do that and leave me sitting out in the lonely desert wondering what in blazes the news was?

Three days later, I visited Henry. I had my ticket for the next day's stage, all my business was completed, and I had nothing to do but wait now. He did not appear especially depressed that day, and I was encouraged by that, but I never knew if he was putting on a show for me.

"I am still holding out hope for reversal of the verdict during the review process," I said. "Send me a telegram when you hear. I doubt that I will be in a position to receive announcements early enough to beat the San Antonio Daily Express, but my agent has a contract with a half dozen eastern newspapers for my story. I've already written most of one story for any reversal and another for a sustained verdict."

Henry looked at me incredulously. "You have already written stories? Before they've happened?" He shook his head in disbelief.

"It's not that terrible. Most of what I have written is background, although a few quotes from you in advance would be nice to have since I won't be able to talk to you personally." I hoped I would not annoy him by making him aware that I was already writing a story about the possibility of loss. Fortunately, he seemed to find it all rather humorous and joined the game, giving me ample quotes to be used for either ruling.

It was a tough goodbye when I left that afternoon, and I embraced my old friend after wishing him the best. I was confident that we would remain in touch, but I had no idea when I might see him again, or If I ever would. I must confess that tears welled in my eyes, and several escaped, as I walked back to the boardinghouse.

Chapter 39
The Decisions

I T WAS ONLY several weeks later in early January 1882 that Henry received notice of General Christopher Auger's decision, which dampened his hopes of reversal in his favor. In fact, Auger's decision worsened his position. Auger endorsed the verdict that Flipper was guilty of conduct unbecoming an officer and a gentleman but insisted he should have been found guilty of embezzlement.

President Arthur would make the final ruling after receiving recommendations from Judge Advocate General David G. Swain of the Department of Military Justice. In the meantime, Flipper was escorted to the largely isolated Fort Quitman, over one hundred miles southwest of Fort Davis not far from the Rio Grande. It was a small outpost that he had stopped at on various scouting missions.

The adobe structures were crumbling, and he volunteered to help with repair and reconstruction and received no objection. A worthwhile task for a prisoner, the temporary commander decided. Sadly, the commander was Lieutenant Charles E. Nordstrom, now the husband of the former Mollie Dwyer. Fortunately, since Nordstrom's duty was temporary, Mollie had not accompanied her new husband.

Henry did not mind the remoteness of the fort and rather enjoyed the background of the Quitman Mountains, which, although far from towering, provided a contrast to the surrounding desert. This gave him an opportunity to spend time outside and to pay more attention to his three horses in the stable. Unfortunately, he was not permitted to ride the animals outside the boundaries of the fort grounds, and he worried about their getting adequate exercise.

He produced substantial correspondence during this time, writing frequently to Jordy, who was a reliable correspondent. He wrote to Barber for any news he might have regarding the verdict's review. Family members heard from him with regularity, and he made lengthy entries in his diary daily. He recognized that writing was more compulsion than desire for him.

The weeks turned to months, and finally in June, Henry received official notice that President Arthur had confirmed the original verdict. Although the embezzlement charge would not be reinstated, he remained guilty of the charge of conduct unbecoming of an officer and a gentleman. He was released from arrest and discharged from the Army.

With the passing days, hope had waned, and he had already decided about his future. He would not be broken and go into hiding someplace, and he would seek an uncertain future in the Southwest. He selected El Paso as his starting place. His language skills might be helpful there. Perhaps a trained engineer would find work in the growing border town. He had a list of every person who had advanced money to help him at Fort Davis. He had never considered those funds donations. They were debts that must be repaid, and soon.

He needed cash to tide him over before he left the post, so he sold all three of his horses to Lieutenant Nordstrom, the only man who appeared to have funds to make the purchase. Tears rolled down his cheeks when he walked away from Valiant. It especially stung to have Nordstrom assume ownership of his pride and joy. It occurred to him that Mollie might once again ride the stallion someday, and that thought consoled him a bit.

On the last day of June, Henry, having removed the insignia from his uniforms and surrendered the rank and company designations to Nordstrom's office, boarded a stagecoach that would eventually make its way to El Paso. His farewell to the Army was without ceremony or formality of any kind. He departed the post with the clothing and gear he was able to salvage and the grief he would forever carry in his heart.

Chapter 40
Jordy

Taryn told me of the news from the post about President Arthur's decision regarding Henry's case several days before I received Henry's wire confirming it. Of course, the defendant would have been last to know.

Henry advised me not to write since he would be leaving Fort Quitman soon. He promised to write as soon as he established a new address. He did not even mention where he was headed, which worried me a bit. Was he going to return to Georgia, disappear back East someplace?

I felt like I had been caught in a whirlwind since Henry and I parted almost six months earlier. The news that Taryn had kept me in suspense about just before I departed Fort Davis was that she was with child. Our little Stacia was a month old now, a pretty, little gal with prospects of her mother's auburn hair. Thank the Lord, she did not show signs of taking after her father's side.

We have two other children now, also. Taryn spoke to me about it first, and I agreed to take in her brother Herbert's children for a year. His wife had died a year earlier, and he lost the nanny at his previous station to marriage, and she was unable to accompany Major Blair to Fort Sill.

A few months earlier he had been transferred to Fort Robinson in northwestern Nebraska. Taryn had become quite close to the fourteen-year-old daughter Carlie, and the eleven-year-old son Curtis had made friends at Sill. Besides, Herbert had no arrangements for their care and supervision at Fort Robinson.

I had a feeling that the children were likely settled in for an even longer stay given the apparent stability of our living arrangements, and Taryn had pointed out that Carlie could be a huge help with the babies. Yes, she said "babies." That's plural.

I'm glad Taryn found a two-story, limestone house where she could have her clinic in three main floor rooms. We would still have a kitchen and parlor downstairs, and there were five small bedrooms upstairs, She was already talking about adding onto the house to provide for several hospital rooms and an office for me.

The house and a nice stable were set on a twenty-acre tract, and she was set on living out our lives there. That was all fine with me. I could not love the woman more, and I think she liked me well enough. I was just wondering if we were going to fill up those acres with buildings and kids.

Taryn's Army contract was to expire August 1st, and she was being pressed to extend it. Her private practice was becoming all she could handle, however. It included many Comanche patients thanks to a friendship she had formed with Chief Quanah Parker.

It was late, a warm evening, and Taryn was nursing the baby as we sat in the parlor when I told her about my message from Henry.

"I wondered if he had heard," she said. "Daddy and my brothers have always complained about the way news travels in the Army. Official word always arrives last. What now for Henry?"

"He didn't say. He will let me know when he has an address."

"Do you think he will go back east to be near family?"

"No. I'm betting he will end up someplace in the West."

"Speaking of the West, how long do you think it will be before Jack Winchester's book is released?"

"Any day now, according to the agent. I told you that he received the five-hundred-dollar advance. Of course, he takes twenty per cent. He will wire the money to our bank account before the week is out. I should finish the next book within two weeks. I don't want to be kept around just for stud services—although that's not a bad task."

She looked at me and smiled. "Well, my stud will need to wait a few more weeks, and then I've read of some scheduling we might follow to maybe put off another child for a bit."

"You've got a schedule for everything, don't you?"

"I'm not so good at following it with my stud, though."

I should explain. I am Jack Winchester, author of a new dime western novel. I am contracted for one every two months, and with luck I can make a living sitting on my butt. I am doing some ghost writing for others, too. Memoirs for politicians and military folks. I will still write now and then under my own name, but those novels are the easiest. Imagine getting paid for telling lies. I suppose my autobiographies for the politicians sort of do that.

Anyhow, Taryn and I were doing fine near Fort Sill and committed to a life there. It appeared that we would not starve, and there was a chance we might be able to afford all those projects she was devising for our property.

Chapter 41
Jordy

FOR THE REMAINDER of that year, I heard frequently from Henry before his missives lapsed for a spell. He ended up in El Paso along the Mexican border, which made sense with his gift for Spanish. Translators are in demand in those areas of mixed cultures.

His first letter reported that he had found work in a laundry office but was vague about what he did there. With the second letter two months later, he enclosed articles he had written for the *El Paso Times* as well as several stories written by the publisher, Marcellus Washington Carrico, defending the dismissed soldier and praising him. Henry had obviously found a friend.

With two jobs, Henry wrote that he was able to start paying his debts to those at Fort Davis who had helped him erase the shortfall. With that letter he enclosed a draft for the amount of the loan Taryn and I had made with interest precisely calculated. We had never expected repayment, but we knew it would injure his pride for us to turn it down.

He seemed to be meeting a fair number of people and mentioned there were many former Buffalo Soldiers in El Paso, and that colored folks were generally welcomed into the community. Many of the former soldiers had taken Mexican wives, although because of Texas's anti-miscegenation laws, Henry doubted that the marriages had been formalized.

As he understood it, those of white, Indian or Spanish descent could freely intermarry, but none could marry a person of Negro descent unless it could be proven that the prohibited ancestry was multiple generations back. Henry wrote that he had tried to calculate the allowable taint in accordance with the statute and found it a challenge. And then how would one prove his or her lineage? He seemed to find the law more a tribute to ignorance than anything else and was unconcerned. He was not interested in marrying anyone, but since such marriages carried the potential of two to five years in prison, he supposed he would arrange for marriage in Kansas if the issue ever arose.

That was Henry. He was aware of injustices and would sometimes speak out against them but never allow such things to keep him from carving his own trail through life. He was never popular with most colored leaders because he was never inclined to be their public martyr.

He especially upset some Negro rights groups when he objected to congressional legislation that would allow Negroes to enter West Point based upon testing standards lower than those mandated for whites. He suggested that the proposal was condescending and insulting and would be an affront to those colored people who met the standards. The legislation died in committee, but he lost allies who might otherwise have supported him during the court martial.

Henry's correspondence was rather bland during his first year in El Paso. He kept the laundry and newspaper jobs until mid-1883, when he gave up the laundry and commenced doing some survey work for business folks who had become aware of his expertise. I really thought at this point he had decided to nest in El Paso, but I was wrong.

In the fall of that year, Henry wrote about a new opportunity. An American company owned entirely by former Confederate officers obtained a concession in the Mexican state of Chihuahua to survey public lands there in exchange for one-third of the surveyed land. The company employed an engineer named A.Q. Wingo to command the surveyors. Henry had met the man when he was scouting for the Army and had helped him with a few surveying jobs near El Paso.

A. Q. Wingo insisted that Henry be hired as his assistant. He knew Henry to be a competent surveyor, but he also wanted someone fluent in Spanish with him. The company owners protested at first because of Henry's race, but Wingo informed them they could hire another supervisor if Henry was not joining him, and that quickly resolved the issue.

Henry explained in this letter that I might not hear from him for some months since he would be in Mexico for a time and would be moving through Chihuahua far from any post office. He promised to write when he settled for a spell someplace in the United States, more than likely El Paso. After reading that letter, I caught a touch of wanderlust, speculating on whether I might try to catch up to Henry and join him for a spell. I was cured that night when Taryn informed me she was with child again.

Chapter 42
The Mexican
Adventure

ENRY WALKED ACROSS the bridge spanning the Rio Grande that took him into Juarez on the Mexican side. His telegram advised that he was to meet Wingo at a wagon yard in the town of Chihuahua located about two hundred miles south of Juarez. Wingo had informed him that this morning would be the last day for a week that he could board a stage in Juarez for the journey to Chihuahua.

When Henry saw the stagecoach, evidently rehabilitated from an old Wells Fargo coach, he immediately had doubts that the rickety structure could survive a seven-days journey. He met Pedro, a congenial Mexican driver, white-haired and wrinkled like a prune who explained that he would need to hitch his duffel and bedroll to the stage top. The wizened man was glad to see that Henry carried a rifle and pistol and was obviously pleased that the colored passenger spoke his tongue.

When Henry saw the other passengers boarding, he figured English would not be necessary for this journey. As they prepared to depart behind three two-horse teams, he saw that the boy riding shotgun could be no more than sixteen; he could see why another gun was welcomed.

"My grandson, Rafael," the old driver explained when he saw Henry studying the boy. He knows how to use his weapons." He went on to explain that the stagecoach was one of three used in their family business, and that his sons were occupied with the other two today.

He had already been warned that it was dangerous for a man to travel alone through that country because the area was infested with bandits waiting to move in and steal a man's money and personal belongings, and, of course, his horse. Generally, the traveler's body was left behind for the buzzards.

There were four other passengers, two businessmen and their wives. They enjoyed pleasant conversation, and Henry learned that one of the men was a banker and that the other was an entrepreneur engaged in many enterprises. Both seemed interested in his surveying project and expressed hope that this would stimulate interest in establishing railroad connections.

They ate well enough at houses along the way. Sleeping accommodations were limited, however, and he spent most nights in his bedroll under the stage. He did not take offense. He understood that when only two bedrooms were available at the small adobe houses used for stopovers, the ladies and their spouses should be granted priority. Besides, Pedro and Rafael shared his outdoor accommodation.

Henry often rode shotgun while the boy napped on top of the stage. He had volunteered for the duty because he sought opportunities to stretch his long legs after enduring the cramped coach. As they approached Chihuahua City, he asked Pedro about the location of the wagon yard and learned it was on the south edge of the town and that he would take him there after they dropped off the other passengers.

As they rode through the town's dusty streets just before noon, he noted that there did not appear to be any hotels or restaurants, although taverns were ample, and he supposed a man could grab something to eat there.

Hopefully, he could locate Wingo quickly, and his boss would direct him to an eating place.

The wagon yard off the end of the main street was easy enough to locate with its vast lot filled with wagons of every sort, and he was fortunate to see Wingo talking to a Mexican man outside one of the six stables. The stage pulled in, and after thanking the driver and grandson, Henry retrieved his belongings and climbed down from the stage top. Wingo caught sight of him; he smiled and waved him on.

Wingo was a stocky man of average height with a full, short-cropped beard and thick eyebrows the color of ripe wheat. Age-wise, Henry guessed him to be in his late thirties.

"Henry, you are just in time," Wingo said. "Ten words of Mexican just ain't enough to make a deal." He stepped out and shook Henry's hand. "I've been chomping at the bit to get our job on the way, but we've got to get a crew and wagons and mules first."

"Good to see you, Wingo. I'm ready for some steady work." Everybody called the engineer by his last name, and Henry had no idea what his initials, "A. Q.," stood for. "Maybe you could introduce me to your friend."

"Oh, yeah, I should do that." He turned to the Mexican, a small, white-haired, mustachioed man who studied Henry with a suspicious look in his dark eyes. "This is Carlos Aranda. He owns this wagon yard and everything that's in it." He looked at Aranda and nodded toward Henry. "This is Henry Flipper."

Henry extended his hand and the Mexican accepted it, but he still had a wary look in his eye. "Buenos tardes, senor Aranda." Then, speaking Spanish, he explained that he was from El Paso and would be working with Wingo.

The man relaxed noticeably, and they agreed to call each other by first names. Aranda began to tell Henry more than he wanted to know about the wagon yard business, but he did not interrupt, certain that it would help their cause to be an attentive listener. He just smiled and nodded agreeably, occasionally asking a question that elicited a long answer.

Finally, Wingo's patience wore out. "Find out what it's going to cost to buy two wagons—both covered—two mule teams for each and the tack."

Henry explained to Aranda, and the man responded at length. Henry turned to Wingo. "He wants to know if you can pay in American gold."

"Yeah, everybody wants gold down here. The value of Mexican paper bounces up and down so much—mostly down—they never know how much money they've got.

Find out how much he wants, and then we'll work on cutting him down some."

Half an hour later, Wingo owned two wagons and eight mules. Aranda also agreed to find six men, including one with some cooking skills, who would accompany and assist the surveyors.

Wingo turned to Henry, "Hungry?"

"Starving."

"There's a Mexican lady that serves up good food at her house just down the road within walking distance. I've been taking meals there, so she'd be expecting me. Needs the money, so she'll be glad for another guest."

"My bedroll and duffel?"

"Follow me to your sleeping place. We'll share a lodge."

When they arrived at the adobe lodge on the edge of the wagon yard, Henry saw that it was one of five identical structures in a row, each lodge about twelve feet by twelve feet square. They stepped in, and Henry found it was furnished with an oil lamp on a windowsill, nothing else. He sighed and dropped his gear on the dirt floor. "At least, tonight I'll have a roof over my head."

"Probably the most luxury you'll have for a few months. We're surveying the east boundary of the entire state of Chihuahua and then larger tracts west of that along the way. Might come across a few adobes where somebody will put us up in a barn, but mostly it's on the cold, hard ground. Tomorrow, we go shopping for supplies. We might find some tents if we're lucky. The weather can turn dang cold this time of year, too, so we should be looking for some long underwear and sheepskin coats. Extra blankets might be good. I hope to pull out the next day, so we'll be busy today and tomorrow."

That was fine with Henry. He was paid for surveying days, so he was ready to get started on his new job. "I'm fine with that. Where do we start?"

"We'll head south to the southeast corner of the state and work our way back. Have you seen maps of the area?"

"Yeah. Everything I've seen is darn crude. Put two maps together, and the boundaries don't look the same."

"We are to fix that. Our maps will make the geography books."

"It appears Chihuahua abuts the state of Coahuila to the east, so I assume we will be establishing that state's boundary as well."

"To the extent it adjoins Chihuahua. Durango to the south has been surveyed and approved by the government. We should be able to locate the point where that state's northeast corner intersects with Coahuila's southwest. Then, we head north from there to the Rio Grande maybe three hundredsome miles. Something else I have not mentioned."

"Yeah?"

"If the Mexicans like what we do on this job, the company will likely be hired to survey the west boundary that connects mostly with Sonora."

"I don't have a list of other jobs waiting."

Wingo said, "You will when this work is completed, I guarantee it."

Chapter 43
Death Visits

TWO WEEKS AFTER their departure from Chihuahua City, Henry and Wingo had finished surveying for the day, when they saw swirling, black smoke climbing into the sky. Wingo was driving the mules for one of the wagons, and Henry sat beside him on the seat. Wingo signaled a stop to the wagon following him and reined in his mules.

Wingo said, "That's no grass fire ahead, and there ain't enough trees in these parts to make a forest fire."

"No," Henry said. "Buildings burning, maybe a house."

"I don't want to drive into trouble. I doubt if it's Indians this far east these days, but there's plenty of outlaw bands working these parts."

"It can't be more than a mile away. Let me take Felipe and we'll hike up that way and see what's happening. Give us a good lead and bring the wagons slow-like. We'll be running fast toward you if we've got to set up for a fight."

The Mexican crew split up and rode in back of the wagons when they were moving any distance, and Henry hollered for Felipe, whose face appeared from the opening in the wagon canvas behind him. "Yes, Henry?"

"Grab your Winchester." He pointed toward the smoke. "We're going to see what's going on down the trail."

Henry snatched up his own rifle and stepped down from the wagon, and the wiry Felipe stood on the rock-strewn arid ground beside him in an instant. The two moved out ahead of the wagons at a fast walk. Henry had come to count on Felipe during their days on the surveying trek. He was the tallest man in the group, but still three or four inches shorter than Henry. A thick, black mustache aged him some but he was not more than a few years older than Henry. He spoke English more than passably, having worked as a cowhand on the northern side of the Rio Grande and even scouted for the Army in New Mexico and Arizona for two years.

Felipe had been visiting family in Chihuahua City when he took on the surveying job, figuring he would work his way back to El Paso, where he was courting a young woman he hoped to marry soon. He worked hard, and Henry thought he was quite intelligent. He figured Felipe would do just fine on either side of the border, but it seemed that his lady friend, a birthright American citizen, had no intention of moving to Mexico.

As they moved toward the smoke, they darted for brush cover and paused whenever they had the opportunity, surveying the landscape ahead. Henry pulled his spyglass from its holster on his belt and pressed it to his eye. When he had the instrument focused, he did not like what he saw.

"No riders," he said, "but there are bodies in the yard, at least one woman." He handed the spyglass to Felipe. "Tell me what you think."

Felipe was silent for some moments, his mouth grim as he studied the site. "House burned to ground. Barn, too. We must go and see if there are any who can be helped. Bandidos. These people out here have nothing worth stealing. Some just like to kill. They take two, maybe three, horses. No time for cows. They could steal without killing, but such men have a sickness."

Henry stepped out onto the trail and waved the wagon drivers forward, and he and Felipe hurried toward the smoking buildings. They quickly confirmed what the spyglass had revealed. A young man and woman lay sprawled out in the yard, the man's body riddled with bloody holes like he had been used for target practice.

The woman was naked below the waist, telling Henry that her death had likely been slower than that of the man, presumably her husband. No bullet wounds. Her throat had been cut when they were finished with her.

He scanned the yard for other victims and saw a baby not far from the burned-out door of the fire-gutted adobe home. He could see that the child was dead, its skull having been caved in, but he rushed to the baby's side and knelt. The face had virtually vanished amidst crushed bone and mangled flesh, but the blanket that had once cocooned the baby was wadded in the dirt nearby, and the nakedness revealed a boy child, probably not more than a few months old.

Henry retrieved the blanket and wrapped it around the baby.

"Nothing more than animals. Those vermin ought to be put down."

Henry looked up. Grim-faced Wingo was standing a few paces behind him.

"Why?" Henry asked. "Why would anyone do this?"

"I can't answer that. There are some bad ones in this world. Some days, it seems like there's more of them than decent folks, but that ain't so. There's lots more good than bad. I like to think so anyhow."

Henry sprang to his feet. "I guess we've got work to do. The least we can do is give these folks a decent burial."

"I'd say a common grave. That way they can all be together. I'll get Emilio and Javier to work on it."

Henry cast his eyes toward the smoldering wood pile that had been a barn or stable. "What's Felipe doing over there?"

"I don't know. He's been meandering about with his nose to the ground like a dang birddog. He scouted the Apache for the Army, you know. Maybe he's trying to pick up sign. Go ask him. God knows why, but he's taken a liking to you from the start."

"I think I'll do just that."

When Henry caught up to Felipe, the Mexican was staring at the ground, rubbing his chin thoughtfully. "What are you looking at Felipe?"

Felipe pointed to the loose dirt in front of him. "What you see there?"

Henry studied the ground for a moment and then he saw what Felipe was talking about. "Tracks. A child's, I think."

"Little girl. Footprints everyplace."

"So these folks had another child."

"Si. Bandidos take."

"Why didn't they kill her like the others?"

"Money. They take two horses. Girl bring more than four horses. They will sell her."

"To a whorehouse?"

"Si. Some men like little girls. She will spend life there. Die young."

Henry was sickened by the thought of a little girl being held by such men. "We've got to do something."

"I will follow and free the girl."

"You can't do that alone. You would be facing a whole gang."

"Three men. That's what tracks say. They be stupid men. Not like Apache. They leave maybe hour before we come. Blood not dry yet."

"But they're on horseback. I will go with you, but our mules must rest and are not likely broken to riders anyhow."

"We walk. Men not go far. Maybe hour or two from here. They think nobody find bodies for days or weeks. They make camp. We ride back on their horses."

Felipe had obviously been thinking about this and had a plan of sorts. "I'll talk to Wingo. He won't like it much, but he needs to set up camp, too. The sun will be setting soon. There is a well here. I'll suggest he find a suitable place nearby, and we'll be back before sunrise, so we won't miss a day's work." Unless they were dead.

Chapter 44
Pursuit of Justice

DARKNESS SHROUDED THE barren land by the time Felipe and Henry had been separated from the others for a half hour. Wingo had not been pleased about their intention to pursue the killers, but when Henry told him of the fate that faced the little girl, his heart softened, and they left with his reluctant blessing. "What are we going to do with any prisoners you take?" Wingo had asked.

Felipe had said, "There will be no prisoners."

Henry worried that with the darkness, Felipe would not be able to track the abductors, but five horses left ample sign for nose, feet and eyes with dung apples dropped along the way. Even with lapses of such clues, Felipe had no difficulty filling the gaps because the riders were making no attempt to hide their trails. What fools would dare follow them anyway?

They had been walking for nearly two hours when Felipe stopped. "Do you smell that?"

Henry had not, but soon after Felipe mentioned it, his nostrils picked up the faintest odor of smoke. "I do now. Smoke."

"Camp is near." His eyes searched the desert-like landscape scarred with dry gulches and toothlike hillocks rising from the flatlands. "Other side of spiny ridge."

The moonlight was ample this night, and he could see the ridge Felipe had identified. It erupted abruptly from the tableland reaching no more than a dozen feet and extended no more than fifty feet before disappearing underground again and looked like the back of a giant reptile. It ran east to west and would make a nice windbreak from a north wind that was picking up. He chided himself for not wearing more than his buckskin jacket tonight.

For the first time, Henry offered his thoughts. "Why don't I just go around the end of that ridge and march right to the camp. I'll sing a song, and that should befuddle them some. I'll wait for you to get to the top of the ridge to sight things out. You wave when you figure out how you are going to go about this, and you're positioned where you want to be. Then I'll start my show. I should be able to see you."

Felipe cocked his head to one side and looked at Henry as if he thought his friend was crazy. "Dangerous for you. Not so much for me."

"You just take down whoever is closest to the little girl. Or if she's not there, you come back down, and we'll talk about it. We could both just shoot from the top of the ridge, but I think somebody needs to get to the girl fast if they've got her."

Felipe shrugged and started for the ridge. He scrambled up the rocky incline like a mountain goat and studied the scene below him for several minutes before he waved. Henry took a deep breath, and with his rifle cradled in his left arm, walked around the end of the ridge and toward the campfire that the men were hunkered around. At first, he did not see a little girl but then he spotted her curled up at the base of the ridge, probably more than fifteen feet from the fire but fortunately on his side of it. She wore only a thin dress and had to be freezing.

The outlaws had not seen him yet, but he began to sing "The Battle Hymn of the Republic" as he walked toward them. They doubtless would not understand the words, but he liked the song and knew it well. He had been told he had an outstanding voice, but he had never given the remark any credence, not that it would make any difference here.

The outlaws got to their feet and just stared like they were seeing a ghost. Felipe's first shot cracked, and a man toppled into the fire. Henry raced toward the girl, his Army Colt clutched in his right hand. One of the abductors saw him and raised his own pistol to fire. His shot went wild, and Henry took his time, aimed and placed a slug in one of the man's eyes, dropping the man instantly. Felipe fired two more times, and the third man joined the others on their trip to Hell.

Speaking Spanish, Henry stepped over to the little girl and knelt beside her and said softly, "You are safe now. We are here to help you."

She just looked back at him, her lips quivering and eyes terror stricken. He figured she could not be more than five or six years old. He had little experience with children of that age and was uncertain how to approach her. He was rescued by Felipe who was sliding down the slope.

"Felipe," he said when his friend righted himself at the ridge's base less than ten feet from him, "I think the girl is frightened of me. I suspect she has never encountered a colored man."

"Very possible. I talk to her. She see terrible things, I fear."

"I will collect the horses and saddle three. There's a big knapsack not far from the fire. I'll see what these men have in the way of valuables and things worth salvaging and dump it all in there. We'll want to take their guns for sure. Maybe these things can be sold and used for the little girl somehow."

"That I leave to you." He went to the little girl and began speaking very softly to her as he sat down beside her.

Henry first retrieved a few of the blankets laid out for bedrolls and took them to Felipe. Then he emptied the pockets of the bandidos, gathering a fair amount of Mexican paper money as well American gold coins, mostly twenty-dollar double eagles, probably the product of earlier thefts. He discovered the knapsack was already nearly one-third full of watches, jewelry and more gold coins. He assumed these men had left a trail of dead bodies behind during their ventures.

He saddled the horses and shoved the rifles in the saddle scabbards and assumed that the three best animals had belonged to the killers. The other two horses were big, but lower quality critters, probably used more often as a wagon team and for farm work, although he could not imagine what would grow on this godforsaken land.

The bodies would be left for buzzards and other scavengers just as these men had intended for the young Mexican couple and their baby. There was a time when Henry thought everyone was entitled to a decent burial. His thoughts about many things were changing as he experienced life.

When the horses were saddled, he joined Felipe, noting that his friend now cradled the girl in his arms. "I've done all I can. Are you ready to ride?" Henry said.

"This is 'Camila.' I have explained that you are her friend, too. She will ride with me."

Henry said, "Hola, Camila." He continued in Spanish, "Yes, I am your friend, also. You may call me Henry. You are safe now."

Shortly, after Henry lifted Camila into the saddle of Felipe's mount and she was settled between his arms, he mounted a sorrel gelding, and they turned back on the trail that had brought them to the slaughterhouse.

Chapter 45
More Work

CAMILA HERNANDEZ REMAINED with the survey crew until nearly Christmas when they reached the Rio Grande and completed surveying the east boundary of the state of Chihuahua. Henry was uncertain about where and when his duties would end, but he was pleased that after his weekly payment in gold, he would have sufficient funds to pay the balance of his debt to the Fort Davis merchants and still be left with enough money to tide him over for several months. His West Point engineering education had not been wasted.

They were a day or two from Juarez, where they would put up the mules and arrange storage of the wagons. Wingo approached Henry the night before they would follow the Rio Grande west to their destination.

"Henry, would you tell the men that we will pay their remaining wages when we get to Juarez. There may be more work, but we will not know for a month. Tell them they have done a good job, and we would be glad to hire them on again, but those who are willing and able will need to stay near Juarez or El Paso and tell us how to find them. We can notify them either way when we know."

"Yes, I can do that. What about the maps?"

"You and me will go across the river to El Paso to the company office there and make up three sets of maps from the surveys. That will take us several weeks. The company has arranged for a courier to take one set to the officials in Chihuahua City. They will be contacting the company with any questions. Hopefully, they'll say quick-like if they got more work. Would you be willing to take another trip?"

"Yes, I need to stay employed at something."

"Well, this would be to the west line of the state, and, again, parcels in that area that will be for sale less those to go to our employer, the Harrison outfit. There are some mountains there, and some renegade Apaches still show up now and then I'm told."

"I've fought Apache before, and I wouldn't be looking forward to it, but most are on the reservation these days I understand."

"Most, but not all. Something else."

"Yes."

"Camila. We've all sort of adopted her. What do we do with her?"

The thought of abandoning the girl to an orphanage or strangers tore at Henry's heart. "She's most attached to Felipe. They're almost like father and daughter. I'll talk to him, but I'm betting he's got plans in his head."

"The horses and tack, all the money and such those outlaws carried, that should go to her care," Wingo said.

"We don't have any argument there."

Later that evening, following his announcement to the crew, Henry asked Felipe to speak with him. "Felipe, Wingo and I have talked about what happens to Camila when the crew breaks up. I'm hoping you have some ideas."

"Maria and I marry as quick as can be done. Camila be our first child."

"But you haven't discussed this with Maria."

"If she is person I believe her to be, she say yes. If no, then I not marry, but still make place for Camila with me. Not worried, though."

"You can sell all the horses and tack and take money and other things we collected from the outlaws and help set up a home for the girl."

Felipe's brow furrowed. "But I did not earn it."

"You are taking it for Camila. It won't begin to pay for what she lost."

"No, what you say is true."

"It's settled then."

After arranging for care of the mules and wagons in Juarez, Henry and Wingo moved on to El Paso to work on the maps. They found decent hotel rooms there, although Henry conceded that he had lowered his standards some during his journey over the past several months. It was almost six weeks before they received word via telegram that they were employed for another surveying job along the western boundary of Chihuahua. The assignment was irresistible to Henry because his proposed salary had been doubled.

Chapter 46
Jordy

I T HAD BEEN months since I received a letter from Henry, and his latest was pushing to match the length of one of my dime novels. This missive assured me that, indeed, Henry had not been broken by his unfortunate discharge from the Army. He was preparing to join Wingo on another surveying trek, but said he had many surveying and engineering opportunities ahead.

This did not mean he was finished with the Army. His debts paid, he employed legal counsel in the East to pursue his case in the courts and congress. He wrote that so long as he took a breath, he would not end that fight. Regardless, however, he was committed to utilizing his skills wherever they might find a measure of satisfaction and source of sustenance.

The surveying job with Wingo on the western side of Chihuahua took almost all of 1884 and 1885. The mountains and Apache uprisings rendered the surveying long and tedious. Although they had no direct encounters with Apache, Henry wrote of the discovery of the mutilated bodies of a family of five, who had been killed only hours before the surveying party's arrival. He lamented the inability of the Mexican and American governments to forge peace by this time.

After the Chihuahua projects, Wingo and Henry went their separate ways, and Henry did independent engineering work for Mexico, Texas, New Mexico and Arizona, never lacking work for even a day. In 1888, he was interviewed for a story by J.D. Ponder, editor of the El Paso Times, a bizarre coincidence since Ponder's father had once owned Henry and his parents in his and Henry's native Georgia. Ponder wrote a convincing story asserting that Henry had been the victim of other white officers who had planned and carried out a scheme that would result in the colored lieutenant's dismissal from the Army. I must note, however, that no substantial evidence of such a plot was recited.

In the early 1890s, Henry made a visit to Fort Sill during a return trip from Washington, D.C. where he had been summoned to discuss a possible government appointment. Taryn and I were thrilled to see him and convinced him to stay with us several nights. By this time, we had four children, her brother's children having grown and moved on with their lives. Curtis was in his final year at West Point, and Carlie was a schoolteacher and married to a first lieutenant currently assigned to Fort Riley, Kansas. Our children were Stacia, age ten, Jacob Jordan, more commonly called JJ, age eight, Nancy Ann, age five, and Henry Robert, age three.

The children all loved Henry and would not leave him alone. His namesake especially took to the visitor and spent many hours on his lap. I wondered then if Henry would ever marry, perhaps have a family of his own. Surely, he had gotten over Mollie Dwyer by now.

I was making decent money with my writing projects now, still turning out dime novels for steady income, ghost writing for some politicians and submitting articles to newspapers and magazines. I contributed more than half of the household income from my fees and royalties, and I had come to accept that most outsiders did not look upon writing as "real work." Taryn's opinion was all that mattered, though.

The first day of Henry's visit was spent on leisurely things, such as a walking tour of Fort Sill, which I sensed still held a special place in his heart. He even mentioned that he envied my being able to live nearby. He was still Army, always would be. He got acquainted with the kids that day, but the next day the three older children were in school, and we had time to talk.

It was a balmy day in the early afternoon of late March, and we sat on the front porch. Our home faced east, and although the veranda's roof shaded us some from the sun, we enjoyed basking in the warm rays, and young Henry napped on Henry's lap.

Henry said, "You've done well, Jordy. Somehow, you've managed to keep a spell over that wife of yours. She still loves you. Her eyes tell me that."

"I think she might and sure know I got a prize when she consented to marry me."

He smiled and chuckled. "It took a conspiracy to get you to ask."

"I'm grateful you helped with that."

"I find all your books whenever I return to civilization. If you add more pseudonyms, be sure to tell me so I can keep up. I'm sure I don't see all your articles, and, of course, you can't reveal the books you've ghosted. Anyhow, you've got the gift. The characters in your novels have a depth that I haven't seen in any other books. I'm sure that's a big draw to your readers."

"I don't know. I'm just grateful I can crank out a living putting a bunch of words on paper. I'm not smart enough to write the stuff you do."

"Don't be so modest. I get paid little or nothing for the things I write. Most folks find my work boring as blazes."

"I'm sure we have very different audiences, but I'm curious, you are stopping here after a trip to Washington. Do you have a new job? I realize it's none of my concern."

"No secret. As you know, I've been in Nogales several years now, working with lawyers on claims arising from the old Spanish land grants. The town hired me originally because the whole town became subject to the claims of people who alleged they owned every property in Nogales by reason of being successors to the original holders of the grants. I established by study of the documents, all written in Spanish, and a complete survey, that all the claimed parcels were located in Mexico."

"That must have made a lot of folks happy."

"Yes, and it led to a lot of other work, some of it for the United States government. I have now been appointed as special agent to the new Court of Private Land Claims and will be paid ten dollars daily. My job will be to study and analyze land grant documents—many of those recorded in Mexico—and to conduct legal surveys where required. This should be a reliable income for some years."

"I'll be danged. I'm really glad for you Flip."

"Of course, my lawyers back east will take a chunk of that. I'm encouraged that they are gaining support in congress for action that would exonerate and clear me of the court martial charges."

"Is it worth it? You have proven yourself to be a man of integrity and skill. The court martial is known to everyone, but those who work with you and come to know you don't give a dang. Who cares?"

"I do. There is nothing more important to me than a reversal of that decision."

I just shrugged. I had written and published many articles about the injustice that I believe was done to Henry that fateful day. I knew of nothing else I could do.

It was with great sadness that I saw Henry board the train the next day, wondering when our paths would cross again. I would have bawled like a baby if I had known then that this was to be our last face-to-face meeting.

Chapter 47
Jordy

ENRY AND I continued our correspondence during the years after he departed Fort Sill for the last time, and I often learned of his activities from the newspapers. More than once, he caused a public stir when he criticized the Democrats.

He had always been a staunch Republican and voted for that party's presidential candidates, with the notable exception of Democrat Grover Cleveland who returned to office after an intervening term by Republican Benjamin Harrison. Henry wrote that Cleveland was more fiscally prudent than Harrison and more dedicated to the respect of government limitations imposed by the Constitution.

Henry could not refrain from writing periodically of his political views and tended to light the flames of public controversy from time to time. But one man's villain is another man's hero, and his views likely opened a few more doors than they closed.

Henry spent most of the 1890s working as special agent for the Court of Land Claims, interpreting Spanish language documents, surveying and testifying in court regarding correct locations and validity of the land grant documents. When he was not working for the land grant court, he contracted for private surveying work. Later in the decade he was also appointed as Deputy U.S. Mineral Surveyor.

As the 1900s began, he left the Court of Private Land Claims for a position as resident engineer of the Balvanera Mining Company in Ocampo, Chihuahua and lived in that Mexican city for a half dozen years, making frequent visits to American border towns and often meeting with the company president, William McAdoo, in El Paso. McAdoo would later become Secretary of the Treasury.

Henry loved his time in Mexico and made many friends there. He often wrote of his adventures and social interactions, seeming not quite like the shy, nonsocial Flip I always knew. He stayed in that country until the Mexican Revolution pushed him back to the United States. He settled in El Paso again and took positions with several mining companies. During this time, he became acquainted with Albert Fall, who at the time was a Santa Fe resident and attorney general for the territory of New Mexico. Upon New Mexico being admitted to the union as a state in January of 1912, Fall was elected to the United States Senate from the new state.

Fall was a major investor in one of the mining companies and was impressed with Henry's proficiency in Spanish and his experiences with the Mexican government and that country's people. He also became chairman of the senate foreign relations committee and pressed Henry to join him in Washington. Henry hated to leave the Southwest but had passed sixty by this time and was enticed by income and nearness to family.

He remained with the committee until Senator Warren G. Harding was elected president and Senator Fall, a loyal Republican, was appointed Secretary of the Interior. Henry was immediately appointed special assistant Secretary of the Interior at an annual salary of $3,000. Several years later when Fall resigned, Henry left the position and was approached by William F. Buckley, Sr. for a position as engineering and legal consultant in Venezuela for Buckley's company, Pantepec Petroleum Company.

Henry reported that he was paid well and that he was finally accumulating some cash and good investments. Then the stock market crash of 1929 triggered hard times for the company and decimated his savings. At age seventy-five, he returned to his roots in Atlanta, Georgia and the home of his brother, Joseph Simeon Flipper, who was a Bishop of the African Methodist Episcopal Church. He was pleased, however, when Pantepec employed him for translation projects and engineering advice that could be accomplished from his bedroom office in the home there.

Our correspondence slowed during his years in Venezuela, and after his return, I was distracted by other concerns. Taryn lost a three-year battle with cancer in 1933, and her absence haunted me whatever I was doing. Thankfully, both Stacia and JJ had followed their mother into the medical profession and were already managing the new hospital that had been constructed on our land. I know it gratified Taryn to see her children carry on her dream and mission, not to mention the pleasure of the herd of grandchildren nearby.

Young Henry became a West Pointer of all things. A captain now, he was committed to an Army career which worried me some with the war brewing in Europe. It would most certainly involve the United States no matter what our politicians vowed. My old friend Henry was pleased to learn of my younger son's career choice and insisted on regular progress reports.

And Nancy Ann lives in Santa Fe with her lawyer husband and three children. She studied journalism and takes special assignments from the Santa Fe newspaper. She has also taken over one of my pseudonyms and is writing and publishing western novels. The old dime novel has died, but there is huge demand for such books these days. The old west Flip and I lived continues in print and on screen, much of it not so realistic, perhaps, but entertaining and engrossing to the followers. Those of us who went through those times are thinning now, and it is likely Henry Ossian Flipper and Jordan Dixon are nearing the end of the trail. For whatever time I've got left, I will just be grateful for the special people, including Henry Flipper and my darling Taryn, with whom I got to share my life.

Author's Commentary

Henry Flipper's Story Continues

Henry Flipper died May 3, 1940, at the age of 84 shortly before the war he had been predicting commenced. He was a prolific writer, much of his work consisting of letters and articles commenting on political issues of the time. In addition to his West Point memoir, Flipper wrote another book in 1916 which he never tried to publish. The manuscript was discovered in the Atlanta University library in 1960 after being donated by his relatives. The book, edited by Theodore E. Harris, was later published as *Black Frontiersman, The Memoirs of Henry O. Flipper*.

The book, an important source for this novel, includes some of Flipper's later correspondence and commentary by the editor that gives further insight into the thinking and character of this exceptional man. The editor and the letters recite Flipper's consistent opposition to President Franklin Roosevelt's New Deal. Flipper quotes Adam Smith's defense of capitalism, and Harris comments that Flipper would likely be quite comfortable with the economic writings of Thomas Sowell and the late Walter Williams of more recent times.

Whatever one might think of his views, Flipper, Booker T. Washington, and other like-thinking black figures of the time were not popular among a significant number of black people in the late 1800s and early 1900s. As today, folks of a particular race or skin hue did not always speak with a single voice.

Regardless, Flipper never ceased his efforts to clear his military record. Up to the date of his death, isolated representatives and senators attempted to assist by congressional action, but support was lacking. Many thought the issue was irrelevant because of the passage of so many years.

Redemption

Finally, after World War II, Congress determined that all matters pertaining to appeals of court martials would be delegated to the Army Board of Corrections of Military Records. In 1976 an application was filed on behalf of Flipper's nephew, Festus Flipper, and niece, Irsle Flipper King, asserting that Flipper had committed no criminal act and that his punishment had been too harsh. After a hearing, the board, which had no authority to grant a full pardon, ordered that the record should be changed to show that Flipper was separated from the Army on a Certificate of Honorable Discharge.

Within a few years after the decision, Flipper's remains were removed from Atlanta, and he was reinterred with full military honors near his parents. Family and admirers continued to pursue a full pardon, however, and President Bill Clinton pardoned Henry Ossian Flipper on February 19, 1999.

After the pardon, a bust of Flipper was unveiled at West Point, and an annual Henry Flipper Award was established for graduating cadets who exhibit "leadership, self-discipline and perseverance in the face of unusual difficulties." A monument to Flipper was installed in Thomasville as well and a post office dedicated to his memory.

The Flipper Brothers

Festus and Isabella Flipper nurtured a remarkable family that included five sons. Henry, of course, was the eldest, and much of his story has been told in the preceding pages.

Joseph, born in 1859, is mentioned briefly in the novel and served as a college president and bishop of the African Methodist Episcopal Church. Festus Jr., born in

1868, remained in his father's leatherwork business, but had great business acumen and engaged in farming and other businesses as well, eventually becoming a wealthy landowner.

Emory, born in 1873, became a medical doctor, practicing in Jacksonville, Florida, and Carl was a longtime professor at Savannah State College in Savannah, Georgia.

Historical Fiction

This is a work of historical fiction. Most of the dialogue is the product of imagination, of course, and some of the events less relevant to the course of Henry Flipper's life are conjecture or outright fiction. Jordy and Taryn are fictional characters, but most of the officers and others involved directly in Flipper's life history existed. The author has attempted to stay true to the essential story of this complex man.

Acknowledgments

Special thanks to Len Powell, a former mayor of Thomasville, Georgia, who first made me aware of Henry Flipper's roots in that community. Len later put me in touch with folks who helped me tremendously with my research.

I am grateful for the assistance of Ephraim J. Rotter, curator of the Thomasville History Center and Sarah Byrne, museum educator of the Jack Hadley Black History Museum in Thomasville. Ephraim and Sarah were both very helpful in providing me with voluminous information about Flipper's background and life story. Their kindness and generosity will always be remembered.

The following books and publications were valuable resources in writing this novel:

Jane Eppinga, HENRY OSSIAN FLIPPER: WEST POINT'S FIRST BLACK GRADUATE, Republic of Texas Press, 1996

Henry O. Flipper (Compiled and edited by Theodore D. Harris), BLACK FRONTIERSMAN: THE MEMOIRS OF HENRY O. FLIPPER. Texas Christian University Press, 1997

Henry O. Flipper (Introduction by Quintard Taylor), THE COLORED CADET AT WEST POINT: AUTOBIOGRAPHY OF LIEUT. HENRY OSSIAN FLIPPER, U.S.A. University of Nebraska Press, 1998

Charles M. Robinson III, THE COURT-MARTIAL OF LIEUTENANT HENRY FLIPPER, Texas Western Press, 1994

Kay Johnson Haugaard, AN OFFICER AND A GENTLEMAN, Brad Haugard, 2023

Krewasky A. Salter, THE FLIPPER BROTHERS, The Urban Voice (article), 2011

About the Author

Ron Schwab is the author of several popular Western series, including The Blood Hounds, Lockwood, The Coyote Saga, and The Lockes. His novels Grit and Old Dogs were both awarded the Western Fictioneers Peacemaker Award for Best Western Novel, and Cut Nose was a finalist for the Western Writers of America Best Western Historical Novel.

Ron and his wife, Bev, divide their time between their home in Fairbury, Nebraska and their cabin in the Kansas Flint Hills.

For more information about Ron Schwab and his books, you may visit the author's website at www.RonSchwabBooks.com.